BLACK ROSE:
BITTER SWEET

EMBRACING FREE LOVE

YASMINE RUSSELL

Lightning Fast Book Publishing, LLC

P.O. Box 441328

Fort Washington, MD 20744

www.lfbookpublishing.com

The author of this book tells a fictional story of a young runaway slave woman who is torn between romantic interests. The literary offering provided is fictional and derived from the imagination of the author. The intent is to give readers a captivating read. In the event that you use or enact any of the material in this book, the author and publisher assume no responsibility for your actions.

This is a work of fiction. All characters and events are fictional.

The publisher, Lightning Fast Book Publishing, assumes no responsibility for any content presented in this book.

ISBN-13: 978-0-9994653-7-0

ISBN-10: 0-9994653-7-6

TABLE OF CONTENTS

DEDICATION/ ACKNOWLEDGEMENT

This book is dedicated to all those whom have loved and lost or found a reason to live. I dedicate this personally to all those whom I have loved and who always believed in me. My mother Ruth, who always told me, "If you want it, then go get it," and has always directed me to follow my heart. To my father, Michael Russell, for loving me until the end (RIP). To my Uncle Kosmond and Uncle Skip who loved me from the moment they knew of my existence, and whom no matter what have always seen the best in me, even at my worst times. To my Spirit Sister Allie; thank you and I was blessed to have met you. You mean the world to me. To all the men who loved me through my life, je t'aime aussi, you just were not the one. I am sorry that I cannot name everyone at this time, but you know who you are. I hope that this book can entertain and give hope to those around. Love can distort judgment, but can also make you recognize the right thing to do. In addition, I must not forget Ms. Marion Williams (Tina-Marie) and Mr. Dick Altree who made my gloomy childhood bearable. I wish that when I had grown up, you both were alive to see your positive influence on me. May you both RIP.

CHAPTER 1

The night air was cold upon Mona's skin, but she pushed on trying to avoid the thoughts swirling around in her head. She didn't want time to pass her by and so needed to be alert at all costs. One slip up and it could cost her, her life. She recalled to earlier in the day when she began to pack her belongings and bid her mother and friends farewell. They told her to be safe and careful and not to ever look back. They told her they loved her and wished her well. She would always be in their thoughts and prayers and she told them the same.

Mona placed some cooked rabbit and cornbread in a cloth to take with her for the journey. She crept slowly out of the slave quarters being careful not to wake a soul. It was so quiet that you could hear a pin drop. Mona was nervous and scared, but she knew what she must do. This was no life for her, and she vowed she wouldn't die without tasting freedom.

She tiptoed to the big barn where the fastest and most prized horses were kept. She figured it would be faster, because either way, in the morning, they would find her missing and be on the hunt for her. Mona decided the punishment, if caught, would be the same, so why not do her best to gain more ground.

She knew the strongest and swiftest horse well. After all, she spent endless hours conversing with him when she had no one to talk to her. She only had a few friends as most of the other slaves resented her because she retained her wholesomeness. She guided the horse carefully to the edge of the road making sure no one had seen her. Once in total darkness, she jumped on the horse and rode like her life depended on it, for it did! She rode on to her new life, scared and hopeful all in the same breath. Mona rode and rode until she could barely keep her eyes open. She knew she had to gain as much distance as she could and find a safe place to rest. She wouldn't worry about those who would be hunting her until she absolutely had to, so she kept pushing on.

In the morning, Master Russell decided he wanted breakfast in bed, so he called in the kitchen staff. "Have Mona bring my breakfast," he belted. Privately, he thought that he might just have her for breakfast, as he had waited long enough for her to become a young woman. He had kept his promise to her mother, and now the time had expired. He hungered for Mona, and he felt that only she could quench his desire.

Master Russell fantasied about how beautiful Mona's brown skin was; she was short, but he liked short women. She had an unspoken beauty, her eyes were an odd brown, and he had never seen such eyes. Moreover, she was very curvy and that pleased him immensely; he is glad he waited for her to fully mature. Her hair was not like the other slaves, not as nappy, but thick and it smelled heavenly. He felt his groin tighten as he thought of Mona and he was more than eager to release his seed into her whether she was willing or not!

Master Russell screamed, "Where is Mona with my breakfast? I don't like waiting! One of the servants slid into his room, "She is gone Massa, I can't find her" the elderly woman trembled. She stepped to the side and said a silent prayer as Master Russell sprang from his bed buck naked in anger with his manhood displayed for all to see. For an older man, Master Russell was built like an ox with salt and pepper hair that fell in soft curls to his shoulders. He had piercing, green eyes that burned with fire. He had a rugged appearance, which held the interest of all the single women in town. After his wife died in a carriage accident with their youngest daughter, Master Russell vowed they were irreplaceable and kept his word. Mona was going to be an exception, but he would just make her his concubine.

Master Russell grabbed his clothes and yelled for his boys "Michael! Dennis! Get your butts in here, now!" It sounded more of a growling than English. The boys came running in to make sure their father was okay. Michael was the first to arrive, "Yes father, what is it?" Dennis followed in with a slow strut, "Yes father?" Dennis could care less what the issue was; he was being interrupted from his morning festivities.

Michael was tall at 6'0", well built, with light brown wavy hair and piercing green eyes. He was very athletic, handsome and he had a smile that had all the women swooning. Many of the women in town would receive his courtship, but Michael was fussy, and his heart was claimed by another. Michael and Mona had grown up together; they were inseparable as children and shared a birthday as well.

Dennis was a few years younger than Michael was; he was short, at approximately 5'9" and athletic just like his big brother. He was stocky and handsome as well but not like his brother. Dennis had Sandy blonde hair and blue eyes. Michael and Dennis were both well-educated and well-traveled due to the family business. These young brothers were high-class society and every single woman in town desired them. Master Russell chimed up, "Mona has run away, and we must go find her! I want her back now!" he yelled. He was filled with rage. To Master Russell, Mona was a prize he wanted all to himself.

Master Russell remembered how he had to send Michael away to boarding school because he and Mona had gotten so close and it sickened him. He didn't want anyone in his way, not even his own son. The three men headed downstairs to gather a few more men and the horses, Master Russell aimed to get his prize back!

Mona ran all night and spent most of the next day dodging everyone and everything in her path, stopping for nothing. She would take small catnaps here and there when she felt semi safe. Mona knew she had to create as much distance as possible. Lacking sleep, she knew she needed more rest. When it got dark she placed the horse down by a creek, walked a few miles, found a tree, and climbed as high as she could and got comfortable enough to get a little rest.

Mona was awakened in the early morning by the sound of a young girl. "Hello" the little voice said. Mona stayed still, she thought she was hidden well enough and thought that maybe the girl was calling out to someone else. The voice called out again, "Hello, wake up sleepy head, it is morning time!" she looked Mona dead in the face and smiled. She jumped down from the tree and backed away from the girl slowly. Terrified Mona spoke up, "I'll just be on my way ma'am; I don't want any trouble."

She smiled again, "Well you don't want to sleep the day away silly. C'mon," she gestured for Mona to follow. Mona was confused and distraught. Mona looked the girl up and down as she followed her; they had to be close in age. The girl had beautiful brown hair, big bouncy spiral curls, and big brown eyes. She was dressed as she held a status and her mannerisms were comforting. She turned to Mona and said, "My name is Ruth, and you are?" I am Mona" she smiled shyly. "Do not be afraid, I will not hurt you Mona", she grabbed her arm and pulled her along.

"Where are we going? Mona asked uncertainly. Ruth smiled whole-heartedly, my parents are out so we are going to my house, where I will bathe and feed you. Then you can be on your way, Ruth giggled. Mona just let Ruth lead her and hoped for the best. They had done everything that Ruth said that they would do together. Mona developed a fondness for the girl. Ruth perked up, her face full of joy and happiness. "I am getting married!" Ruth could hardly contain her excitement. "Congratulations!" Mona squealed excitedly, she was happy for her new friend.

Ruth excitedly told her, "His name is Michael Russell!" Ruth held her heart as she described her fiancé to Mona.

Mona turned to Ruth, "I wish you the best, but I really must be going!" Ruth walked her back to the spot she found her, and Mona didn't have much to say. Ruth bid her farewell and they wished each other the best.

Mona hugged Ruth and fled quickly; she ran to her horse and bolted! After hours of riding, she finally stopped early in the evening. She had to stop; her body would not let her continue. As soon as she came to a halt, her body shut down and the tears flooded her face soaking the horse's mane. Her heart screamed in pain as she felt her soul shriveling. "Michael!" she cried out even louder, "How could he?" Mona felt the true sting of heartache. All she wanted was to die; this was the only man she had ever loved. Mona had yearned for this man for what felt like a lifetime. Moreover, within a few hours, every ounce of her strength had disappeared. She thought back to happier times, when the innocent love they shared was real and hope kept her alive.

(Flash Back)

"Mona, my father is sending me away; he doesn't want us to be together anymore!" Michael held Mona's hand tight, "I love you" she kissed his lips. "I will wait for you; however, I don't think you will wait for me!" Mona let her hand slip out of his. Michael pulled Mona to him, gazing deep into her eyes. "I will always be yours, no matter what happens, even if I cannot marry you, my heart will always be yours. My soul will always be intertwined with yours; no one can change that! Not Ever!"

As he kissed her forehead, they were interrupted. His father called out to him, "Michael, let's go, let that nigger be!" Michael hated how his father spoke about Mona. Michael kissed her passionately, "My love is always yours, no matter who or what tries to come in-between us." He released his grasp and Mona pleaded once again, "Michael, I love you and I will wait for you!" she wept as his father dragged him to the waiting carriage, laughing.

Mona had not seen Michael in about a decade. She had finally seen him a few days ago, when he arrived home. Oh, how she had missed him, she had waited and waited for this day. When he arrived, her face lit up with joy and her heart was overflowing with love. He walked past her as if she was a stranger not even a glancing at her. Mona felt the sting of rejection deep within her being and that's when she knew she had to leave. She would die free, free from slavery and free from heartbreak. Mona lowered her head as tears stung her face. She tried to hide them from the others, who thought she was naïve in thinking he really loved her.

(Flash Back Ends)

A noise brought Mona back from her thoughts and she noticed she was near a lake. Mona heard a noise again; it was the sound of splashing water. Mona peeked from behind a bush where she sat. She gazed in awe, she had never seen an Indian warrior, but she had heard stories about them. She wanted to get a closer look, so Mona crept around the lake to find a good spot in which to watch him. She found a small boulder that she could lean against and rest. She lay there watching the Indian warrior in the water, his long dark hair fell to the middle of his back, and she thought it must be so soft.

Just as Mona sank deep into thought the Indian warrior emerged from the water buck naked, Mona's eyes widened as she'd never seen a naked man before. As she lifted her body to get a better look, someone pushed her from behind down the hill and into the water. The Indian warrior paused to watch, Mona did not know how to swim so she started to panic. Just then, Mona was lifted out of the water and she became hysterical. Mona turned to look and she saw it was a white man that had pulled her from the water. Mona tried to get away but he held onto her tightly, "Sorry, I didn't know you couldn't swim." he laughed heartily. "Name's Greg", he continued to chuckle. "And this is George." as he pointed to his friend.

Mona noticed George held a rifle to the Indian warrior, "What do you want?" she tried to turn away. George grinned, "Looks like we now have two prisoners and this one I'm sure will get money for returning". Mona spoke up, "How can he be your prisoner?" "Never you mind," and grabbed her tighter pulling her along. George asked, "Why don't we just let her go?"

"Have you gone soft? With her we will surely get money and a soft bed to lay upon". Greg looked irritated. Mona remembered the horse she had hidden away; they hadn't noticed him. She just needs to get to him and she will be free again. If she can get to her horse, this nightmare will be over. However, how could she get to the horse? She knew the first chance she got; she would take it no matter what happened! The men were on their way to hunt and to bring Mona back. Michael stopped at his fiancée's home. Ruth stepped out with a great big smile from ear to ear. Michael immediately jumped off his horse to greet his future bride. "How are you dear? I have missed you." Michael kissed her hand. "I have missed you as well my love," she smiled coyly.

"Enough with the chit chat, have you seen a female nigger running this way?" Russell yelled. "Why no sir, I have not." she lied innocently. "Michael, may I have a private word with you?" Ruth tugged on his arm with a serious look on her face. Michael grasped her hand and led her away from the search party. They were still in view of the other men when they stopped to talk. "Is everything alright?" He looked deep into her eyes. "Why yes, it is, I met a slave girl named Mona this morning, is that who you are searching for?" she asked curiously.

Michael instantly becomes nervous as he feels his heart sink into the pit of his stomach. "I fed and bathed her. She kept me company briefly. I knew she had to be one of your slaves because when I told her of our marriage, she was in a hurry to leave." Ruth informed Michael. "She must have thought I would turn her in, but you know I am against slavery." she watched his eyes to gauge his response. His face showed devastation.

Michael was utterly sick to his stomach; his fiancée had aided the love of his life to gain her freedom. All the color drained from his face; he looked as if he had seen a ghost. His true love had met his soon to be wife and it was too much to take in at once. "Your secret is safe with me." he kissed her cheek "We must go." he hurried to join the search party swiftly mounting his horse.

They rode for a while and as darkness started to set in, they agreed to stop to make camp and eat supper. After supper, Michael went to lay down; he had a lot on his mind and no one to share it with. All he could do was think of Mona; he missed her so much and longed to hold her tight. He wanted to tell her how much he loved and longed for her; but he didn't and couldn't. He had to keep up the façade that Mona meant nothing to him so he did not alert his father. He did not want his father harming her. Michael decided to come up with a way to keep her safe and all to himself.

Michael did not want to marry Ruth because Mona had his heart completely. But his mother thought the match was a wise choice because she knew Mona held her son's heart, but it could not be so. Mona and Michael was an unacceptable match and would not be wise nor safe for either of them. She had wished for this marriage all those years ago when Ruth and Michael had first met. To honor his mother in death, he had promised to marry Ruth, and he would whether he loved her or not.

Ruth was beautiful, smart, and she had a heart of gold, but she did not compare to Mona in his eyes, nor his heart. No one else compared to Mona and never would. Michael's plan was to marry Ruth and keep Mona at his side by giving her a room in the house. Michael wanted only to sleep with Ruth to consummate their marriage; otherwise, he wanted nothing more to do with her. Michael directed all his love, loyalty, and devotion to Mona; he couldn't wait to start a family with her. Michael dreamed about the life he would have with Mona as he slowly drifted off to sleep in peaceful bliss.

As the night air cooled, they slept in peace. Michael woke up abruptly calling out for Mona; he had a nightmare that he had lost his love. His father heard his cries and instantly became angry at his sons' childish outburst. "Damn it Michael, are you still pining over that nigger?" Michael jumped to his feet to challenge his father's comments only to see Ruth was watching. Michael started to speak but held his words and anger back. His father grabbed him by the collar, pulling him close "Let me tell you something son, when we find her, I'll finally break her in and make you watch." Russell let Michael go and laughed with a sinister laugh they had never heard before. Michael stormed off as his father laid back down to go to sleep.

Michael found himself pacing the ground, thinking that he would kill his father before he ever allowed him to hurt one hair on Mona's head. She meant more than life to Michael. He finally tires from pacing and went back to camp to get some rest. He prayed to God that he would find her before his father did. He would hide her out if need be. With his mind made up, Michael fell back to sleep.

CHAPTER 2

Mona found herself sitting on the wagon as they tied the big Indian warrior to a tree, so he couldn't escape as they slept. "What about the Girl?" George piped up. "She'll sleep in between us and if she tries to escape we'll feel her, besides she's not dumb enough to try." Greg belted out laughing with a hint of daring in his remark. They made a pallet on the ground to get some rest; they had a long day and were exhausted. They decided to "take advantage of Mona after a goodnights rest." Mona lay there for what seemed like hours; she couldn't sleep, she was terrified of what the morning would bring. Mona knew that she had to make a move and soon for her life and freedom depended on it!

Mona slowly eased up on her side and extended her arms pushing herself up. She was in no way strong, and she had only once chance and she had vowed not to fail. She put one leg over the sleeping man trying her best not to touch him. The men started to snuggle closer and with one last thrust, Mona was free! Mona stood upon her feet and started to step away from the sleeping men to her hidden horse. Mona took one look back and felt for the Indian warrior tied to the tree, he looked tired and worn out. She could not leave him to just sit there and suffer.

Slowly heading toward the Indian warrior, she began to untie him from the tree. His eyes fluttered open and she placed her small finger against his lips to keep him silent. The warrior nodded as she removed the ropes from him. She grabbed his arm leading him up to the horse that she had secretly stashed. They walked the horse awhile to make sure it was clear then they both jumped on, riding as fast as they could to get out of the face of danger. Mona was exhausted so she fell asleep against the back of the Indian warrior.

Mona woke up late the next day to find herself in some sort of shelter; she abruptly sat up and looked around to find the Indian warrior sleeping across the way from her. Mona crawled slowly over to him; his beautiful jet-black hair was spread out on the blankets. She longed to touch it, she slowly guided her fingers through it, and as she had thought, it was as soft as silk. Mona placed her hand upon his cheek, she remembered the sight of him naked, and she smiled blushing. Suddenly, he opened his eyes and jumped to his feet. The warrior stared at her for a moment then he left abruptly silently leaving her alone, returning later with an older woman.

He finally spoke to Mona, "I am Wild Heart, and this is Flower Fairy, my mother." "Thank you little one for saving my life." Wild Heart's tone became somber as he turned to Flower Fairy, spoke in his native tongue, and she scurried out. "I am Mona," she said softly, not knowing what to say. Mona sat quietly and waited. Soon Flower Fairy returned with some food and a beautiful native beaded dress. They sat and ate together quietly, and then Flower Fairy took Mona to wash and change clothes.

After dressing, Mona was on her way back to the tepee and was stopped by a woman about her age. "I am Blue Star, Wild Heart's woman, and I thank you for saving his life." Blue Star struggled to smile but then left as quickly as she came. Mona walked into the tepee to see Wild Heart waiting for her, so she decided to speak "I met your woman Blue Star," Mona smiled. "How dare you?" Wild Heart became angry, "She is not my woman!" Mona approached Wild Heart slowly, "I am sorry she told me that she was your woman," she touched his arm to comfort and soothe him. Wild Heart's angry face softened, "You are forgiven, what do they call you?" he asked trying to smile and make conversation. Mona openly giggled; she had spoken too softly, so this time she spoke up. "My name is Mona" thinking did he forget? She looked him dead in the eyes.

"We shall camp here for a few days; you will be safe. My mother has already left for camp, this land belongs to one of our brother tribes, and they let us stay with them often when traveling. "My camp is three days ride so prepare" Wild Heart actually smiled fully this time.

Night had fallen when Mona and Wild Heart lay down to sleep. It was so cold that Wild Heart suggested they sleep close together for warmth. "We should lay close together to keep each other warm," he said as he stood over Mona. However, Mona resisted and insisted she would be fine. "No, I will be fine but thank you," she rolled over and Wild Heart went to lay back in his spot. "Suit yourself." Sometime during the night, the chill in the air became blistering cold and Mona woke instantly. She sprang to her feet and dragged her blanket over to Wild Heart. "Wild Heart, wake up and scoot over," she took the blanket off him to lay it out flat. Mona lay down next to him covering them with her blanket and tucking herself in tight. "His body is so warm," she thought and snuggled closer, falling asleep.

That morning Michael had been awakened by Ruth. "Hello sweetheart, I am coming with you," she smiled. Michael sat up "This is no place for a lady"! Russell got up laughing, "Let her go if she wants to, she'll learn a lot," he smiled coyly. Michael knew exactly what his father meant, and he gave him an ugly glare. "So be it!" Michael stormed off in anger; his father was more than pleased now.

When Mona woke up she was in Wild Heart's embrace and she loved the feeling of waking up in someone's arms. She watched him sleep for a while and when he opened his eyes, she was still gazing at him. "How long have you been laying here?" Wild Heart asked softly. "Well it got so cold, I couldn't sleep, so I lay down with you, but I have only been awake for a few moments," she smiled.

Wild Heart touched her face "You are delicate like a rose, I shall call you Black Rose," he hugged her tight. They were laughing and being playful with each other, and then Mona snuggled closer to Wild Heart. In that moment, Blue Star walks in and gives Mona a nasty look. "How dare you sleep with my man!" she glared at Mona with hate in her eyes. Wild Heart stood up to face her; "You are not my woman, and what do you want?" Blue star never broke eye contact with Mona, "Never mind and black girl, this is not over!" She stormed out. Mona gets up, "I better get bathed" Mona said and then rushed from the tepee. Wild Heart was confused and did not know what to think of what just happened; he was now a little worried. Wild Heart had never experienced jealousy in this manner.

When Mona returned, she noticed that Wild Heart was not around, so she sat in the tepee waiting for his return. It seemed like forever before Wild Heart returned. Mona had awakened to the smell of food. Wild Heart had made her something to eat. "Black rose, wake up, and eat" he looked distraught but tried to smile. Mona looked into his eyes and knew something was wrong. "Wild Heart what is wrong?" she touched his hand.

"The chiefs want to keep you as a captive," he looked away from her gaze. "I am supposed to look after you, and make sure you don't leave." Mona sat closer to him, "Don't be so unhappy, I do not plan on leaving you, besides I don't know where to go." Mona kissed his cheek. She was attracted to the warrior, and she was okay with that, "I'm just happy being free." Wild Heart wrapped his arms around her, "I'm glad you are not unhappy being stuck with me." Mona felt a tingle in her stomach; she dismissed the thought thinking nothing more of it.

Mona looked confused... "What about going to your tribe?" Wild Heart released her, "We can go there, and they are expecting us." "I am sorry you saved my life just to have yours taken little one." He was sad to tell her the news. Wild Heart looked into her big brown eyes. "We must leave in the morning; we must pack up these things." He stood up and started gathering items.

Michael rode quietly beside Ruth. Russell spoke up, "So Ruth, has Michael ever told you about Mona?" he snickered. "Well, he told me that they grew up together." Ruth stated. Russell chimed in, "Well, that is only part of it; they are each other's first loves." Russell looked to Michael, laughing hysterically. "Why did you not tell me?" Ruth looked sad. "Father, how could you?" Michael turned to Ruth, "I did not mean to hurt you," his scowl softened. "I understand," she smiled.

"Why did you come along Michael?" his father looked at him with loathing. "So, you would not hurt her!" Michael's eyes filled with anger. Dennis finally spoke up, "Why do you care if she is hurt or not?" Michael halted, "She's my best friend and besides she's a lady." Russell and Dennis laughed heartily at the statement, almost falling from their horses. Ruth thought that would be a good thing. "That is very sweet darling," she smiled up at him.

They came upon a small tribe and they were greeted by Blue Star. "What are you doing here?" Blue Star spoke with authority. "We are looking for a runaway slave," Russell dismounted his horse. "So, have you seen her?" Blue Star laughed at him, "Oh, it is a woman?" Michael looked up, irritated. "Have you seen her? She is small, petite, and very beautiful." His eyes filled with hope. Ruth didn't like the way he had described her, she looked away to hide the pain in her eyes. Blue Star chuckled, "Why yes I have, she left with a brave warrior, she is his captive," she pointed in the direction they had headed. Russell spoke up, "She cannot be a captive, and she belongs to me." They quickly mounted their horses, "Let's go," Russell started in the direction Blue Star had mentioned. Blue star stepped in front of him, "I know where they are going, and I will take you!" Michael did not like this woman; Russell pulled her onto his horse and rode off shouting, "Let's go!"

Wild Heart finally stopped to make camp so they could sleep. It had been a long and tiring day. Mona was exhausted from the long ride. She turned to Wild Heart as he was laying down sleeping mats. "What if my master finds me while I'm at your village?" Mona was very worried, but she did not wish to put others in danger. Wild Heart sighed heavily, "They will have to pay for your return unless someone pays a higher price," he looked away. "I don't like the sound of that," she shuttered at the thought. They laid down and Mona knew it would be a long and restless night ahead of her.

Russell had also stopped to make camp for the night, "We better get some sleep, as we have a long ride tomorrow." Michael didn't dismount, "I'm not tired so I will keep going and you can just catch up," he rode off. Ruth was astounded at the treachery in his eyes; she could tell by the look in his eyes that he had truly loved this woman and she did not like it. It made her sick to her stomach. "I will go with you!" she called out. "NO, stay here with them." Michael disappeared into the night; he rode for a few more hours until his body was worn out. Michael came upon a pond and decided he would stop and rest there. Unknowing to Michael, Mona was closer than he had foreseen.

Mona got up after tossing and turning all night, she whispered into Wild Heart's ear, "I'm going to the pond for a swim." Mona crept cautiously to the pond. Michael had heard footsteps approaching so he had hid in the bushes to see if Ruth had followed him, but to his surprise… His eyes filled with tears and his heart leapt with hope and overwhelmed with love for Mona.

Michael stepped out in front of Mona, she did not know whether to run and hide or embrace him. He put his arms around her, hugging her tight "I love you so much," he said as he held on tight to her. Mona broke free from his embrace "You do not love me, and I have accepted that," Mona stepped away from him; she could not look him in the eye. "I am sorry about Ruth." He held his hand out to her; Mona started to cry, "I always knew in my heart you would betray me." Michael grabbed her hand "I only did what was expected of me and you know that!" he kissed her lips. "I love only you and I always will." Mona kissed him back passionately.

Mona pulled him closer to her; "Since we can never marry or be together, I think it is time to get this over with." She pulled off her clothes and lay in the grass pulling him on top of her. They had both waited for years for this moment to take each other's innocence and a wedding day that would never come. Mona knew she would only have this one chance, for she had given up on trying any longer with him. They lay together kissing and stroking each other's naked bodies. Michael was getting ready to enter Mona and take her innocence when they both heard a noise, which brought them back to reality.

Ruth stepped out of the darkness; they jumped to their feet and scrambled to get dressed. Michael hadn't known she had followed him; he was so upset with her. Ruth's face was filled with anger and hurt and tears filled her eyes, "How could you

Michael?" Michael did not know how to respond except to say, "I love her!" and he wrapped his arms around Mona. Mona was petrified, her heart was racing, and she was not sure what to do. Mona knew she'd be in more trouble once Russell showed up. She pushed Michael to Ruth "Go to her, if you love me please leave me be." Ruth spoke up, "I agree, you are to never speak her name again and this did not happen Michael. Let the winch go forever."

Michael knew that it would be best so he hugged her goodbye but before releasing Mona he whispered, "I love you!" As soon as he let her go, she ran to Wild Heart "We must go now, my master is near!" Wild Heart rose to his feet and helped her gather their things and left as fast as they could.

Wild Heart rode in silence; finally, he couldn't hold it in any longer. "Who is that man you laid down with by the pond?" He did not like it. Mona was sad and confused, "The man I loved as a child," she quietly wept against him. "We always thought we would grow up and marry with a family; as we got older, we realized we were wrong." Wild Heart stopped the horse, pulled Mona off, and wrapped his big muscular arms around her so she could cry in his embrace for he understood the pain of love as well. Mona wouldn't let herself be carried away, so she told him "We must be going right away." He helped her back onto the horse and they rode off.

CHAPTER 3

Ruth was up early the next morning watching Michael sleep. Her mind was racing, "he better forget about that nigger!" She had made beans and cornbread for breakfast. Ruth leaned down to kiss Michael to awaken him. Michael opened his eyes smiling then he saw that Ruth kissed him, and he fell back to reality. They were eating breakfast, and Ruth couldn't help but think, "What can I do to get him to love me like that?"

Blue Star was up and moving before anyone else and she had returned when they were finishing breakfast. Russell yelled at her, "Where the hell have you been?" Blue Star gave him a dirty look, "I went to scout the area, and someone was sleeping near us last night but it looks like they left in a hurry." Russell smiled, "I know she is near, let's ride!" They quickly mounted their horse and rode out; Russell was eager to find his prize.

Wild Heart and Mona had ridden a long time without stopping, neither of them had gotten any sleep the night before, and both where exhausted. They finally stopped and settled down to eat. Wild Heart had some cooked rabbit and they both ate hungrily and in silence, but Wild Heart watched Mona the entire time, not taking his eyes off her. Wild Heart finally spoke, "Why are you so important to your master?" he was very curious as to the answer. Mona did not look up, "I am chaste and very valuable; he has been saving me." She gave him a vague look. Wild Heart burst out laughing, "How can that be true, I saw you last night with that man." Mona got so angry that she jumped up, "How dare you insult me, I did not do anything!" She threw her scraps at him and moved a few feet away turning her back to him. Wild Heart went over to her, he knew she was hurting, "Little one I am very sorry, I was joking" Mona stayed silent, so Wild Heart started to gather up their things so they could leave. "Let's go", he demanded, "We need to get going." Mona jumped on the back of the horse not taking his hand, still sulking.

Meanwhile, Michael rode in anger and he was very upset Ruth had ruined his night with Mona. They had saved their innocence for each other. Ruth stared back at Michael and smiled lovingly as she thought, "I'm glad I ruined his night, that's what he gets!" She finally spoke up "Michael are you alright dear?" already knowing the answer. Michael would not give her that satisfaction, he smiled big, "I am fine dear, thank you," he was thinking how he hated her. Ruth knew all too well what he was thinking, he was thinking about that wench. Ruth did not want him to find her ever, at least not alive.

Night was upon again them so Wild Heart decided to stop and make camp for the night. He dismounted and lay the bedding on the cold earth. He then went over and helped Mona down from the horse; reluctantly, she let him. Mona was still very much upset with him and he truly felt bad. Wild Heart pulled Mona to him and hugged her tightly. "I am so sorry little one" he knew she needed to be held after all she had been through; "I never meant to hurt you". All Mona could do was weep in his strong arms as he held her tightly; she hugged him back even tighter. She wished that this had all been a dream and she would wake up with everything just as it used to be. In realization, she had known years ago, but she held onto hope because she had no one else. In fact, most of the men in the slave quarters were not even allowed near her. Wild Heart picked her up in his arms and sat down cradling her in his lap until she cried herself to sleep. His heart ached for her, as her friend, he silently vowed to protect her, as he could not stand seeing her like this. As Mona drifted off, Wild Heart wiped her tears and kissed her forehead laying her down on the sleeping mat. Wild Heart knew when she woke she would be hungry, so he let her sleep and went to hunt their breakfast.

Michael could not sleep, he was both worried, and upset "All I wanted to do was be with my true love," he thought. A single tear fell from his eye, but he didn't want anyone to see him cry nor hear him weep for his lost love. Nevertheless, Ruth heard him and it made her very angry. "Why can't you love me like that?" she shouted. Ruth was beyond pissed and she was extremely hurt. Ruth knew she needed a plan to rid herself of Mona but she was so tired that she fell asleep while deep in thought.

The next morning, Wild Heart was up early making coffee and breakfast, Mona got up, went over to him, and said, "Thank you for taking care of me." She smiled as she touched his shoulder. Wild Heart smiled back, "I will always take care of you little one." His remark embarrassed him a little bit; Wild Heart had to wonder, "Was he having feelings for little one?" He had grown accustomed to her and liked it either way. After they ate they rode out as night approached, they had finally reached the camp. Mona was scared and very nervous, "Will he keep his word and make sure no one harms her as promised?" she thought. Upon arrival, she had seen that they were having some sort of party, the warriors had just returned from a big hunt. Everyone was singing and dancing and it made her feel as ease. As they dismounted the horse, they were greeted by Eagle Eye, and he hugged Wild Heart "This is my brother," he introduced to Mona. Wild Heart turned to Eagle Eye "This is Black Rose, my little one" he smiled. Eagle Eye stared her up and down; he had seen slaves before, but never like her, "What a pretty captive!" he said to his brother as he circled her looking at her. Eagle Eye reached out his hand to her, but she did not take it. Mona was dumb founded, she was unsure what to make of it, and so she stepped behind Wild Heart shyly. "Fine, be that way!" Eagle Eye walked off. Wild Heart turned to Mona, "Let us join the celebration Black Rose." He smiled taking her by the hand and leading her to the main campfire.

Mona stopped walking "No, I don't think so." she hesitated, so he led her to his personal tent and started a fire. "I am not hungry, but you should go to the celebration; I will stay here and sleep." she covered a yawn with her hand. Wild Heart stared at her. "I won't leave you!" he smiled at her. "I won't run away; trust me I am just tired" Mona laid down and got comfortable. Wild Heart was disappointed so he went to join the celebration. Everyone seemed to be having a great time, and that made him happy. Eagle Eye approached his brother, "Is the captive your woman?" he questioned. "No, she is my captive" Wild Heart stated as he walked away. Eagle Eye, curious now, "Brother, does she warm your bed at night?" he chuckled.

Wild heart was getting angry. "She is chaste and will remain that way!" he commanded. Eagle Eye laughed, "If you say so brother", he started to walk away, and then turned back to Wild Heart; "Can I have her?" Wild Heart laughed heartily, "If she will have you…" Wild Heart went to eat, he was starving and the buffalo meat smelled wonderful as it roasted. Next, he went to his mother, Flower Fairy, near the main campfire; she had seen her son coming and grabbed some meat for him. "Eat my son; you've had a long journey" she smiled.

Wild Heart took the meat from his mother and sat down next to her. "Thank you Mother" he kissed her cheek. Looking around "Where is your Rose, son?" she asked softly. "She is resting; the journey tired her." He liked the sound of that, "His Rose".

Mona finally got comfortable as she laid down. She started thinking about how well built and masculine Wild Heart's little brother was. "I wonder if he has a woman," she thought, but then she remembered the sight of Wild Heart naked and she giggled. "Oh how nice his body looked while he was dripping wet. She had wanted to touch his body; her face got warm and flustered thinking about him being naked. Mona felt bad about her impure thoughts; her feelings for him had grown. It did not matter either way she thought, "Why not like Wild heart?" Michael cannot be with her and now this is her home; "Wild Heart will protect her", she smiled. "I'll be a good captive," she thought, as her eyes got heavy.

As Mona was rolling over to get comfortable and fall asleep, she heard someone enter; she couldn't make out the figure with her tired eyes, so she stood up quickly. The fire was almost out, and she could barely see. When the person got closer, she realized that it was not Wild Heart but his brother, Eagle Eye. "What do you want?" she blurted out while frantically thinking. "I have come for you" he smiled reaching his hand out to touch her. "Where is Wild Heart?" she demanded. Eagle Eye came closer, "He is enjoying the celebration." He moved within an inch of Mona's face. "You are very beautiful, dark one," he touched her face. Mona was scared now, she was not sure of what her next move should be; "What do you want?" she demanded again. Chuckling, "I just wanted to touch you," he said as he stroked her hair. Mona felt uneasy and backed away from him. "Leave me alone," she yelled. "You do not find me handsome?" he questioned and pulled her to him, leaning in to kiss her. "You are not the one I want to touch me!" she turned her head abruptly and broke free. Mona ran to the opposite side of the tepee, and now Eagle eye was mad, "Who, my brother? No woman has ever turned me down." The look in his eyes were that of a mad man. "You have no sense," he yelled at her angrily. Eagle Eye reached out to her and slapped her face so hard she almost fell. He stormed out as she got herself together.

CHAPTER 4

The day had also been long for Michael, he had hardly spoken a word to Ruth; he did not want her there. Ruth knew that Michael had been upset but she really didn't care, it was his own fault. After a long day, they finally stopped to rest, Blue Star dismounted, turned to the group and said, "We are not far now, it should be about a day's ride from here and then you shall have your slave back". Michael glared at Blue Star; he hated her and wanted her gone. However, Dennis on the other hand, was quite fond of the woman. She reminded him of their mother by her devious actions and he liked that a lot.

As they laid down their sleeping mats, Dennis crept over to Blue Star, "It is very cold, we should lay together," he smiled at her coyly. Blue Star just stared at him and then agreed; she knew what he had wanted, yet she didn't care. Wild Heart knew of her betrayals before they were supposed to get married. He vowed he would never forgive her. "Why should she care anymore; besides, he took that slave to warm his bed." Dennis came closer to Blue Star and she lifted her dress for him. "Don't look so surprised," she smiled. "You are a man; I know exactly what you want." Dennis kissed her deeply and grasping at her full breasts. Dennis had not yet had a woman; he had been too busy with business, but now was as good a time as any, he thought. Dennis kissed and rubbed every inch that his hands and mouth could reach. "Slow down there cowboy," Blue Star held his face kissing him deeply. Dennis had never been kissed like that and it made him want her even more. He buried his head between her legs, tasting her velvet wetness. Blue Star moaned in pleasure so loud that Dennis had to cover her mouth so the others would not hear them. Finally raising his head to kiss her, he unbuttoned his pants and Blue Star was eager to receive him. Dennis kissed her deeply and plunged his manhood deep inside of her. Dennis had never felt such warmth and softness; it felt like heaven to him and he immersed himself within her embrace for the rest of the night.

As Eagle Eye left the teepee, Wild Heart just happened to notice Eagle Eye had been in there. Disheveled, he jumped to his feet, "Had he touched my Rose?" Wild Heart wondered. Standing firm to meet his approaching brother, Wild Heart glared at his brother, "You did not!" Wild Heart was not happy as he grabbed his brother. Eagle Eye yanked away from his brother's hold and walked off fuming. Wild Heart hurried to the teepee, he found his Black Rose underneath the covers. Wild Heart could hear her crying, "Are you alright?" He bent down reaching for her, and she did not speak. Wild Heart pulled the covers off her, scared of what he would find. Holding onto the covers, "Leave me alone" Black Rose cried a little harder. "What is wrong?" Wild Heart was now very angry. "Did my brother hurt you?" Black Rose let him remove the covers. Feeling ashamed, she would not lift her head. "He only hit me," she wept. Furious, he jumped to his feet outraged, "He will apologize to you!"

Black Rose grabbed Wild Heart's leg and begged him, "No! Leave him be; his pride is just hurt." Black Rose sat up, releasing Wild Heart's leg. He sat next to her, not sure of what he should say about the incident. Black Rose laid her head against Wild Heart's massive chest not wanting to think about anything. He held onto her tightly kissing her forehead. "I will stay with you, little one," and held her tighter. They laid back down together, still wrapped in a lover's embrace. Black Rose could not contain her emotions and curiosity any longer. She turned to face Wild Heart fully. His beautiful black hair spread out across the blanket. Reaching out to stroke him, she asked "May I touch your hair?" He smiled wickedly and with a laugh said, "If it makes you happy." Wild Heart stared deep into her big eyes not breaking his gaze. He could only think of how he wanted to kiss her full lips. Black Rose reached across his face to touch his hair again, but was caught in Wild Heart's gaze and instead placed her small hand against his strong masculine jawline. In that moment, they lost all control and Wild Heart pulled her into him, placing his full soft lips upon hers; Black Rose held him tighter, slowly parting her lips to taste his in return.

As Wild Heart held Black Rose in an embrace, their lips hungered for each other, tasting each other. Wild Heart pulled back trying to hide his throbbing manhood; "I am sorry" Black Rose looked away embarrassed. She was not sure what she had been thinking. Wild Heart pulled her back into him, "Do not be sorry, I am not." He kissed her full lips again softly and seductively; Black rose could not catch her breath, nor could she stop the overwhelming emotions that she held for this man.

Black Rose let out a pleasing gasp, "I do not know what to do," she looked down. He pulled her head up by her chin, raising her eyes to meet his, "Love me!" he said, kissing her deeply and hungering for more. With her emotions running wild, Black Rose broke free from his embrace to say, "Only if you love me in return." Wild Heart grabbed the back of her head kissing her almost in a crushing manner. Wild Heart laid upon her kissing her deeply stopping only to look in her eyes. He could not help but to love her; she had been through a lot and she risked her life for his. "I will protect you until the day I die," he whispered, kissing her slowly down the side of her neck. Black Rose could not control her hands; she grabbed Wild Heart's face in her small hands looking him deep in the eyes and said, "Don't ever let me go." She pulled him back down to her kissing him hard. Black Rose kisses Wild Heart with a passion she never knew she had deep within her. She takes in his bottom lip seductively, while sucking and nibbling on it. Wild Heart clutched her small hand kissing and sucking every one of her fingers. Black Rose is so excited she is unsure of what is coming next. This was something she had never experienced and others in the slave quarters had only been with the master, so she had never heard of this. Black Rose felt her body increase in heat; she ached for his touch. Sitting up Black Rose took her dress off and Wild Heart stared in shock, he wanted her very badly, but he wanted her to be sure because he knew her heart at one point had belonged to another. "Are you sure about this?" he asked as he tried to cover her body. Black Rose moved the covers and crushed herself into him, "I want you to be mine forever." She grabbed his neck and kissed him deeply; she could taste blood in their kiss. Wild Heart laid her back kissing every inch of her body; he left no spot untouched. He teasingly kissed her from her lips and down her neck; he uses his tongue to encircle her nipples, slowly sucking on them. By this time, Black Rose was on the edge and couldn't wait any longer; her body needed his. Black Rose grabbed his loincloth, pulling him closer as she spread her legs. "Wild Heart I need you," she whimpers. Wild Heart chuckles biting his bottom lip, he wanted more of her, but he wanted her first time to be remembered. Wild Heart seductively removed his lion cloth; Black Rose eyes widened in shock, but her body was eager. Wild Heart kneeled in front of her, her legs spread invitingly ready for him to pierce her; he grabbed her thighs and pulled her to him, "Are you ready my Rose?" He stared deep into her eyes, "Yes my love," Black Rose said and pulled him deeper into her. Wild Heart does not want to hurt her, so he gently laid on her and kissed her deeply. He plunges inside her and she lets out a painful yet pleasing gasp. Wild Heart looks to make sure she is ok. "Do not stop," she holds him close to her. Wild Heart slowly pushes deeper into her wetness and she grabbed him into her tight embrace. They are locked in a lover's embrace, rocking together in harmony. They made love together all night long as if they were already married. "I love you," he whispered softly. "I love you too," she softly wept. Wild Heart stopped. "Are you ok? Have I hurt you?" Black Rose looked up "Not at all, but is this ok? Is it too soon for us?" Wild heart grabbed her and said, "Not at all, it was your first time." I too had one, but now we have each other, and that is all I care about," he said as he kissed her lips. His words had eased her mind and she kissed him passionately. "Are you ready to go again?" he laughed and then made love to her for the rest of the night. There was no pain only desire for each other as they finally fell asleep at dawn, still connected to one another. Black Rose knew that no one could ever remove her from this man's embrace and that he would protect her, always.

CHAPTER 5

The next morning while everyone was up and going, Dennis and Blue Star were still laying together. Michael had to wake the sleeping duo, "Did you two have fun last night?" he said to the yawning couple. "As much as Wild Heart had with your woman," Blue Star stood up laughing. Michael pushed her back over, "Don't talk about Mona that way!" He was angry and turned to walk away but Ruth followed behind him, "Is that so?" she said turning to walk away. "Ruth, honey I am sorry," Michael ran after her, "It is fine, let's go!" Ruth mounted her horse. Master Russell stood there watching and laughing profusely at all of them. The rest of the men finished gathering their things, so they could leave. Moreover, once the last was done, they rode out together to find Mona.

When morning came Mona realized that she was alone, Wild Heart had left her by herself "Was he angry? Did he change his mind?" Her mind wandered profusely, she did not know what to think. Suddenly Wild Heart returned smiling from ear to ear; he had brought her a red rose. "To symbolize my love for you," he handed it to her and kissed her forehead. "I was worried about you," she took the rose and smiled at his sweet gesture. "There was a meeting this morning that I had to attend to, we have been followed and Blue Star is guiding your master right to us. " That bitch," Mona said under her breath. "They will reach the camp very soon, if they are moving as we presume, they will be here by late afternoon. I will not let them take you!" Wild Heart stood firm in his words to his beloved. Mona stood up and hugged him tightly, "The warriors are preparing for their arrival, and I told the chief elders that I will not let you go, so it has been decided," he kissed her full lips. Afraid, she asked, "Should I run and hide?" Mona was so scared she started to shake, "No, you are not a coward, you are a free woman, my woman!" He left out after speaking sternly. Mona sat down into a ball shape holding herself tightly, she was unsure of what to think. Wild Heart returned with some water for her to drink, she sipped the water in silence. Mona's eyes filled with tears and she finally faced him. "I am afraid", Wild Heart held onto her, "Do not be my Rose, I will protect you." He wiped her tears from her eyes.

"We are very close to the camp!" Blue Star smiled at the havoc she knows that is about to occur, but she doesn't care as long as Mona is not with Wild Heart, she thought, smiling from ear to ear. "Oh, shut up!" Michael blurted out; he really hated this woman. Blue Star laughed in delight, "They will be waiting for us," she glared at Michael. Master Russell trotted his horse over to her, "Are you setting up a trap for us?" he started yelling at her. "No! They spotted us a while ago; you know scouts are always around," she said calmly. Master Russell thought about it, "Well shit!" "Let's load our ammo and get ready just in case they are ready to fight us; everyone load your guns; women included!" Master Russell ordered.

Blue Star laughed at the thought, "Just offer a trade," she said shaking her head. It is simpler than you think. Michael looked at Blue Star "I found our trade" he laughed whole-heartedly because he hated her. "I am not your property to trade!" Blue Star was furious at the idea, what had she gotten herself into this time? At that moment, Blue Star became scared of what might happen next. Master Russell liked the idea his son had talked about. "If we do not get Mona back, you will take her place!" he pointed at Blue Star. Dennis looked shocked, he was not sure of what to think at his brother and father's words; either way, he wanted to keep Blue Star for himself.

Black Rose sat in silence; she looked over at Wild Heart with her big brown eyes swelled up. "How long before you have to leave me?" "We have a few hours." He tried to smile at her to ease her heart. Black Rose went over to him, sat in his lap, and curled up into a ball. "I just want to stay like this forever," she said snuggling into him. Black Rose reached up and kissed his soft lips. "Can I lay in your arms?" Wild Heart laid back and wrapped her in his embrace. Black Rose caressed his massive muscular chest and then she lightly started to kiss his nipples. Wild Heart started to moan, "My sweet Rose." She moved her lips all the way down his hard body, softly kissing him. Wild Heart loved to feel her full lips on his body, there was no better feeling in the world to him. Wild Heart could not take it any longer, "I will love you like no other man will ever love you." He pulled her closer and climbed atop her; he slowly started to undress her and kissed every inch of her body. She moaned aloud "Wild Heart take me," she begged. Wild Heart kissed her soft full lips, "Not yet". He loved the feeling of her small quivering body aching for his. "I love you so much," he stroked her body with his fingertips. She moved with excitement; she yearned for him to enter her. Wild Heart caressed her body and kissed her face, as his eyes never left hers. He finally spoke, "Will you marry me and spend eternity with me?" Mona's eyes widened, "If I am here and we are alive, I will." Wild Heart did not like her response, "Do not talk like that." He kissed her deeply and said, "You have saved my life when you could have left me; I will NOT leave you or let you go!" She took his face in her small hands, "I shall wait all day and night for your return," she kissed his forehead. Mona pulled him in closer and whispered in his ear, "Make love to me." They made love all morning as if it were their last time together.

When Wild Heart and Mona woke up, she felt as if she had slept for an eternity. Wild Heart did not sleep well; he had been more awake than asleep. Mona looked into his eyes; they were angry yet sad. "Are you alright darling?" she asked as she went over to him. Wild Heart snapped out of it, looked back into her big brown eyes. Mona was unsure if he was going to cry or not, "I cannot believe that Blue Star would bring trouble to our people!" His look hardened. Mona touched his masculine face, "I will not leave you my love!" Wild Heart stood up and said, "I must join the others." Mona reached for him, "Not yet!" but Wild Heart pulled away and left her alone; she was so afraid she began to cry.

Flower Fairy entered the teepee and hugged Mona as she had witnessed her tears. "Dear, it will be fine; my son loves you and he will not let anything happen to you." Mona was very worked up, "I don't want him to die over me," she wept hysterically. Flower Fairy held her tight, "He is strong, and he will be fine." She sat Mona down trying to calm the younger woman's fears. Mona didn't find any comfort in her words; she buried her face in the blanket and cried.

The next morning, Master Russell got everything ready and said, "Let's go and get my property!" Michael hesitated but did as he was told; Ruth glared at him thinking, "I hope she gets beat to death," as she smirks. "What are you so happy about?" Dennis interrupts Ruth's thoughts. "Oh just my wedding day," Ruth lies as she gets ready to ride out. "Tie her hands," Master Russell yelled to Dennis as they headed towards the tribe. They don't get very far as they are spotted by some nearby scouts in the area waiting for their arrival. Master Russell looked to the top of the hill and saw a massive warrior. The man made his blood run cold and Master Russell reeked of fear. "He looks like he is ready to kill me!" Master Russell laughed trying to ease his fear. Michael looked up and thought, "That is the one I saw with Mona," and he too shows menace. "Let's go!" Master Russell yelled to the group as they approached the warriors, Wild Heart met them face to face. "Please take me to your Chief," Master Russell smiled. Wild Heart had much hate in his heart for these men, "You have no business here!" he spit. "My slave is in your possession and I want her returned," Master Russell growls. Wild Heart didn't break eye contact, "Well you have one of our women, so keep her, and we will be even." Wild Heart demanded. Blue Star looked at Wild Heart in shock "You actually chose her over me?" she was furious. "Wild Heart, we will see what the chiefs have to say about this!" Blue Star said with rage in her eyes. "They no longer care anything for you after this," Wild Heart snarled. "I am welcome either way Wild Heart, it is law of the land," Blue Star smirked. "Very well," Wild Heart turned and left.

After crying her eyes out, Mona told Flower Fairy, "I am going to the water to sit and think; I just need to be alone for a while." Mona left and headed out to the nearby lake, she decided to disrobe before soaking in the water. The water cooled her warm, overheated body. Little did Mona know she was being watched; Greg and George were standing nearby waiting for the right moment to snatch Mona. Greg and George had secretly met with Master Russell a few days beforehand and devised a plan. They had planned to run in and snatch her as Master Russell created a diversion with the warriors and they would meet up and exchange her for money and land. "This is a fool proof plan," The two men thought excitedly and at the rewards to come.

The two men watched Mona for the right time to grab her, their excitement grew as they crept closer. As she emerged from the water and got dressed, they hit her in the head with a rock causing her to lose consciousness and bleed profusely. "You did not have to hit her that hard," George yelled as he caught her falling body. They wrapped her head to stop the bleeding and drug her to their horses so they could meet Master Russell at the intended meeting spot.

As they made their way into the tribe Wild Heart dismounted and went to speak to the elders and the chief. Chief Long Wind stepped out to greet the party and the traitor that had accompanied them. "I hear you have come for my nephew's wife," The chief said. Full of anger "She is mine," Master Russell yelled. "And I am willing to give you Blue Star in exchange for Mona," he added angrily. "That is for Wild Heart to choose, it is his woman, and I will not interfere!" Chief Long Wind said and left. Wild Heart smiled big, "Now leave, I do not wish to trade". Just then, Flower Fairy ran up to Wild Heart, "Black Rose is gone" she was worried. Master Russell smirked, "Well I guess I will be going". Wild Heart jumped in front of his horse "Wait!" he yelled, "Where is my Rose?" His eyes flashed in anger. Master Russell laughed, "How can I have her? Do you see her? Holding in his laugh, Master Russell stated, "I will be back with the law to retrieve my property." Wild Heart pulled away from Wild Heart and left.

Wild Heart fell to his knees in disbelief, "She said she would never leave," he was confused. His mother Flower Fairy hugged her son as he fought back tears; he broke free from his mother's embrace and ran through the camp looking for her. He could not believe that she had just left. Wild Heart went to speak with Chief Long Wind; "I know that they have her," his heart sank. Chief Long Wind felt sorry for him, but he insisted, "You may not have warriors to start a war over a woman that is not of our tribe," he said seriously. Chief Long Wind placed his hand on his nephew's shoulder. "I am sorry, but I cannot allow this" and excused himself. Wild Heart was furious and not sure what to do next. He went and sat in solitude, he wanted so badly to go after them, but Flower Fairy had forbidden it. Eagle Eye came to comfort his brother, "Maybe she left…" Wild Heart stood with anger in his eyes, "She would never leave me; maybe you helped them take her! You hated that someone loved me first!" Wild Heart glared in his brothers' face. Eagle Eye, upset at his brother's harsh words, stormed off. Eagle Eye had never realized that his brother had felt so unloved until now. Eagle Eye thought, "How his big brother could feel that bad about himself, he didn't know?" That made him more determined than ever to help his brother.

Eagle Eye went out to the lake where Mona had last been seen and their mother, Flower Fairy, joined him. Looking all around they came upon a rock covered in blood, Eagle Eye looked at his mother, and said, "Someone did take her!" Eagle Eye ran to his stallion and left, and Flower Fairy ran to get Wild Heart. However, he was so broken hearted that he wanted no part of it. Wild Heart convinced himself that maybe she had left because he always felt left out and that no one truly loved him.

George held Mona tightly on his horse, "We have to get her help, or she will die." Greg looked at Mona, "Okay, okay! We will just have to meet up with them later." The two men took a detour and ended up at a small town about 65 miles out of their way; they headed to a small farm at the edge of town where they met a married couple and their two daughters. The woman approached and spoke first, "I am Rachel and this is my husband Seth and my two daughters Mary and Elisha!" smiling at the two men. "What can we do for you?" The woman smiled. George spoke up, "Our slave is hurt and she needs a doctor; can you help her?" he had a worried look on his face. Shocked, the woman stepped closer, "Oh yes, of course we can." The two men carried

Mona into the house, where Rachel tended to her wounds. Greg was worried, "How soon can we move her; we must get going?" Just then Seth came around with a shotgun in his arms, "Never!" he aimed it at the two men, "We will not allow you to hurt her again, it's time for you two to get off our property," motioning the men towards the door. Greg became angry, "You cannot just take her from us!" Seth cocked the shotgun as Mary and Elisha came in with gold and handed it to the two men. "Take two of our best horses and never come back or tell anyone where she is." George belted out a hearty laugh, "We just can't seem to keep our hands on this nigger." he grabbed Greg and pushed him out the door.

CHAPTER 6

Mona finally regained consciousness and asked, "Where am I?" She looked around feeling very confused and lost. Rachel ran to her side and held her hand, "You are safe now." Mona was completely lost to her surroundings, "What's going on, who are you, and where did I come from?" Rachel ran to get her husband Seth, "Pa, I think she has lost her memory." Rachel was very worried about the girl.

Eagle Eye searched and searched for Mona, but he was at a loss. He had been wandering around in a circle for days. He knew she could not have gone far, "I have followed this trail, and there is no way she isn't close to this area." Eagle Eye was stumped but determined to find his brother's woman. He finally got tired and decided to call it a night, so he could cover more ground in the morning. Eagle Eye was awakened by a loud thudding noise; he decided to investigate. He saw two men riding horses in a hurry and decided to follow them.

Russell could not wait to get home; he laughed and chuckled all the way and no one had any idea why he was so happy after his failure in getting what he wanted. They rode in silence as his face beamed with joy and happiness. Michael knew that something was wrong, but he could only wait it out with the rest of the group. Russell urged them all to hurry for he had something important to tend to at home. Once they made it home, Russell didn't let his mood break; he held it for over a week. However, after a few weeks his spirit began to diminish and he became angry. Michael and Ruth got married and Russell still had not gotten Mona back, and he was beyond pissed. Russell had held onto his temper long enough and now he had had enough! Russell was so upset he told Michael of the plot that had been in place to take Mona back. However, at this point he had no idea where she could be or if she was even alive. Russell told him about Greg and George; how they were going to bring her back; but he couldn't find either of the two men. Michael was devastated and angry, "You have no idea where she is or if she is safe or alive for that matter!" Michael kicked a table over he was so mad. Russell lowered his head, "No son, I haven't a clue, they all disappeared without a trace." He felt worse for himself than for her actual safety. "Father, this is the lowest point in your life and I hope you're happy," he paced the floor. "I hope and pray that she is safe" Michael began to tear up; he tuned and left the room slamming the door behind him.

Months had past and Mona had finally settled into her new home. Mona had helped the girls make breakfast, "I must speak with Aunt Rachel; I am with child and have no idea who the father is." She was confused but the girls consoled her. "When will my memory return so I have some idea of my past life and my child's father?" she was a bit upset. Rachel and Seth came to sit down for breakfast and they enjoyed every bit of the meal the girls had made, "This was excellent girls, your skills have definitely improved," Rachel boasted. Mona could no longer hold her emotions in and she began to weep, "I'm pregnant and I have no clue who the father is!" she blurted out. Rachel and Seth comforted her and reassured her that it would be ok. "You have amnesia, just be patient and it will all come back to you," they said hugging her tightly.

As the months passed, Mona's belly grew and she became more afraid because her memory had not returned. Eagle Eye finally caught up with Greg and George; he barged in on the two men in the middle of the night. "Have you seen a beautiful black girl named Mona?" He snatched the two men up from their beds. The two men stood while, Eagle Eye held his spear to George's neck; "We do not know what you are talking about!" George started to sweat profusely. Eagle Eye dug the spear into the man's neck, drawing blood, "Yes you do! My brother is dying without his wife!" He let go of George and grabbed Greg piercing his neck with the spear. George broke down and told Eagle Eye everything that had happened; little did they know Michael had been eavesdropping and had heard the whole story. Michael had been set to find the men after his father had told him about the two men on his wedding night. Michael decided to make sure she was safe because his love for her burned deep within his veins. Michael did not want to give up fully and he figured with time she would come around to the idea that they were meant to be together

Michael ran to his horse as fast as he could; he had to get to Mona first before anyone else found her. He was going to bring her home so they could be together and have a family. He knew she would accept him after all she has been through; she knew he was the only one who could keep her safe. George felt so bad at everything they had done; he decided to team up with Eagle Eye to get Mona back. "We will leave at dawn," he told George and then told him to meet him in the woods so they could head out. Eagle Eye did not trust these two men to sleep near him. Greg did not like the whole situation one bit; an Indian stealing away his best friend and turning him good for a woman and not to mention she was not even a white woman, had his best friend gone daft? Eagle Eye went to gather some things and to get Wild Heart. "I know where Mona is brother, she is safe!" he grinned at his brother. Wild Heart looked up at his brother; his face sagged with big bags underneath his eyes. "Give it up, she is never coming back," his eyes swelled up with tears and he laid down turning his back to his brother. Devastated, Eagle Eye left and his mother Flower Fairy was standing just outside. "Mother how is he doing?" he was worried deeply for his brother. "Son, your brother is ill, his heart is weak, and he hardly eats." Flower Fairy was sad for her son.

The next morning Mona felt so much pain she could hardly bear it, she could not move, let alone get up. Rachel came in with towels and hot water smiling at the young woman. "Today must be the big day!" She placed a warm towel on her forehead to ease her pain. Just then there was a loud boisterous knock on the door; the girls scrambled to the door, "Mom, there is a young gentleman named Michael at the door." she hesitated. He was looking for Mona and was wearing a wedding band. Rachel sighed heavily; "Bring him in," she waved. Mona managed to sit in an upright position and Michael walked in with his eyes filled with relief and joy. "How do you know me?" she mustered to say through the pain. Michael sat at the edge of the bed, "We grew up together, and we always wanted to marry each other. We were each other's first love and I am glad to have found you safe." he reached to grasp her hand. Mona moved her hand away, she felt she knew him, but she was unsure of his words. Just then, another contraction hit her hard and he jumped to his feet and kissed her forehead "I love you!" just then she started to remember bits and pieces and the contractions started coming harder. The strongest one hit hard and Michael was unsure of what was happening. Then the blankets fell from Mona and exposed her bare belly. Michael was so stunned that he leapt to his feet in despair. "You're having his baby?" Michael was not happy; he had not expected this. "Wait, it is not your child?" Mona was still slightly confused. "I thought that was why you were here!" she struggled through the pain. "No! I did not know that you were pregnant when my father had you kidnapped!" Michael was so hurt. Mona tried to remember but had to focus on pushing out the baby. Rachel grabbed Michael by the arm, "You have to leave; she's ready to have this baby." After a couple of hours the baby finally came, Michael felt pain for Mona as he heard her screams, so he was glad her pain was coming to an end. "It's a boy," Rachel grinned with joy for her newfound friend, everyone jumped in joy except for Michael. Michael was highly upset that she had given herself to another and bore his bastard;

he was pissed indeed. Just then, Michael came to a knock on the door; it was Eagle Eye, "Where is Mona?" he yelled. "Where is my sister?" He was tired and angry. Elisha ran to open the door "I guess everyone came on the right day" she laughed. As soon as Mona's eyes locked with Eagle Eyes and she remembered everything. "Wild Heart," she cried out. "Where is my love?" her eyes searched for Wild Heart. Eagle Eye ran to her and looked down into her arms at the sleeping baby. "You had a baby?" Mona smiled with tears filling her eyes, "You have a nephew." She handed him the healthy baby boy. Beaming from ear to ear, Mona said, "Wild Heart will be so happy of the news." Her eyes still searched for her love, "Eagle Eye, where is my love?" Tears fell from her big soft eyes. Eagle Eye looked away from her, "He is very ill," his voice trailed off. He has been sick since you left, he did not think you really loved him." Mona did not understand, "Others put thoughts into his head because there was no sign of you being taken, so he assumed you left him." Eagle Eye felt her pain, "I tried to convince him, but he would not listen." "I must go to him!" she cried, and Eagle Eye held her. "No! You must rest." Rachel grabbed onto her and laid her back down, "At least wait and we can talk about it in the morning," She tried to soothe Mona. All she could do was think of getting to Wild Heart; she needed to see him. Mona cried herself to sleep, she was so exhausted, she had slept on, and off for days, only waking long enough to eat and feed the baby. Eagle Eye did not leave his nephew's side; he stayed with him and Mona, so no one could cause them harm.

Mona finally started getting her energy and strength back; she got up and moved around but Wild Heart never left her mind. "Let's go home," she grabbed Eagle Eye as he entered her tent. Tears filled her eyes and Eagle Eye saw the pain in them as she pleaded with him. "We will leave very soon," he walked away as he could not bear to see her pain.

Wild Heart was barely coherent, "My Rose, where is my Rose?" was all he would say. His mother Flower Fairy stayed by his side trying to break his fever, Chief Long Wind came by to see if he had made any progress, but Wild Heart kept going in and out of a dazed state. "Maybe we should plan to send him off to the gods, it seems he is not getting better," he said with a heavy sigh as he left. Flower Fairy held onto her son, "I hope Eagle Eye returns soon," she cried.

Finally, they headed out and Mona could hardly contain the emotions in her heart. Michael stopped her as she headed out to reunite with her love. Seizing her arm, "Please don't leave me." Michael sobbed and begged her to go with him; he would treat her son right and give them the best life. Eagle Eye didn't like this man one bit; with the baby in one hand, he ripped Michael's hand off Mona. "Let her go, she does not want to go with you, and my nephew will never go." Eagle Eye was furious that this man kept trying so hard. He led Mona to the wagon and helped her up handing her the baby, and they rode off. Michael fell to his knees in tears, his life had officially ended, and the only thing he wanted in life did not want him in return. Michael finally got himself together, stood up, and headed to his horse. He vowed never to give up trying; he thought she would realize that she loved him and return; and he was willing to wait a lifetime. It seemed like forever as they rode and rode. Mona thought they would never get there! After a few days, they arrived, and she was so excited, yet sad to see her love in despair; once they had stopped, she jumped off and bolted to Wild Heart throwing her arms around him.

CHAPTER 7

Mona ran as fast as she could to get to Wild Heart. She lost her footing and fell but jumped back up with tears running down her face, she finally made it to him. Wild Heart laid still with no movement, she touched his face and buried her head into his chest crying. Suddenly his hand reached up and held the back of her head. "Wake up my love; I need you" she grabbed his hand and kissed it and placed it upon her face. Slowly his eyes fluttered open, his eyes filled with tears, and they cried together in a lovers embrace. "My Rose," he held onto her tighter, "You are never leaving my side again!" he whispered fiercely. She kissed his lips, "I will never leave you again my love" she helped him to sit up. Flower Fairy came in with food and medicine for Wild Heart; Rose fed him and tended to his needs. "We need to get you better, I have something for you," She kissed his forehead. Once he seemed more stable, Eagle Eye came in to see his brother with a bundle in his arms and he handed it to Wild Heart. "Congratulations brother," he grinned. "What is this?" Wild Heart looked baffled.

Wild Heart moved the blanket and saw a tiny face peeking out; he looked back at Mona and reached for her. "Our baby, my love," She put her forehead to his and he kissed her. "Our son," Wild Heart tried not to cry again but joy overwhelmed him, and his tears flowed. Never had he imagined he would have a family, "I have missed you so much." He kissed her and held her and the baby tight. "It feels as if it has been an eternity since I have been in your arms," she snuggled into his embrace. Flower Fairy came back in to get the baby; "He is still weak, I will watch over the baby." She was so happy to see them together; she left with the baby. Eagle Eye turned to leave, and his brother stopped him, "Thank you, I owe you!" The brothers hugged and Eagle Eye left.

Mona got Wild Heart to eat a little more and move around. She told him about her journey, all that had happened to her, and what happened to her memory, as he hung onto her every word. Wild Heart was amazed that his love had such a hard time and he could never repay his brother for all that he had done for him. When she had finished her story, he looked deep into her eyes, "I love you with all my heart!" he kissed her passionately. "I want to show you how much I love and missed you," he pulled her to him. "You are still too weak," she stroked his long beautiful hair.

Michael had arrived home and Ruth was there waiting at the door for him, and mad as fire. "Where have you been?" she demanded. "Out!" he glared back at her; he was still upset that Mona had refused him; he wanted her and not Ruth. Michael walked right past Ruth; he didn't care to hear anything more she had to say. Michael went to grab a stiff drink. "I said where have you been?" she yelled in his face. Michael was furious, "Leave me alone Bitch!" he pushed her away from his face. "What is wrong with you?" She had never seen him like this, Michael burst into tears and with that Ruth understood what was going on, and she did not like it one bit. Michael's heart was broken and torn and after that moment, he finally felt and understood what Mona had been feeling and going through. Ruth loved him, so she went to him and hugged him tightly. "I don't deserve you or anyone else for that matter," Michael said hugging her back, she pulled back and looked at him "Mona right?" She slapped his face so hard she hurt her hand. "You are my husband!" She walked away to sit down; she couldn't understand why he wouldn't even pretend to love her and that hurt her more than anything.

Without even thinking nor caring, "That should be our baby!" Michael fell back and sank into his chair. Ruth was beyond devastated, "I will be leaving!" She stormed out of the room. "Wait!" Michael ran after her, "I do love you, I care about you! Please don't leave me." He pulled her into his arms and kissed her. Ruth started to cry because she knew Michael was her biggest weakness and it killed her inside. Michael picked her up and carried her to the bed. Ruth enfolded him into her embrace; they had only consummated their marriage, and he seemed cold to her. Michael laid Ruth down on the bed kissing her gently and she loved every moment of it. He slowly undressed her and kissed her breasts, nibbling and sucking on them and it excited Ruth. He took her hair down so he could watch her curls fall around her shoulders. Ruth was thrilled; she reached up and helped him take off his shirt. She began to caress his chest lightly kissing his nipples in return. Michael gets her fully undressed and he wants her so bad that he could hardly hold on. He pushed his pants down and threw them onto the floor. He entered her slowly, but it had been so long since he had been with a woman. Michael began to go hard and deep and Ruth liked this rough side of him. As he went deeper and faster they both began to climax, and Ruth whispered in his ear, "Give me a baby." Michael climaxed and immediately got up not looking her in the face. He grabbed his pants off the floor and jerked them on, "I need a drink," and he left the bedroom.

By morning, Wild Heart felt much better. He and Mona went out for a morning stroll to build up his strength and get him some fresh air. "Let's go get our son." Wild Heart beamed, "I want to get a good look at him," he was very proud of him. They arrived at Flower Fairy's teepee, "Where is my son?" Wild Heart grinned from ear to ear. His mother smiled, "He is with Eagle eye." They walked a little further and found their cooing baby with Eagle Eye; he was telling him stories about hunting. Eagle Eye looked up; "I cannot wait until he is much bigger!" He was so excited about his nephew, "I want a son of my own!" Eagle Eye grinned at the thought of it. He handed the baby to Wild Heart. "What should we call him?" Wild Heart smiled at Mona. He looked at his brother, "Soaring Eagle it is," he chuckled to his brother. "He will go on many journeys as he had already went through many just to get here!" Wild Heart cuddled the baby to his face. Eagle Eye felt a great honor that his brother gave him his name.

They played together with the baby until it was dark, Wild Heart and Mona started to leave, and Eagle Eye stopped them,

"Can Soaring Eagle stay with me a little longer?" Eagle Eye had become so attached to the baby. "Fine; but just for tonight, he will need to come home tomorrow." Wild Heart smiled at his brother and left with Mona to get some rest. Once they had arrived back home, Mona got undressed and went to lay down. She curled up in the warm bearskin blankets and Wild Heart came over to her, and climbed in next to her staring at her hungrily. "I feel much better tonight," he pulled her into him. "I need you right now more than ever!" Wild Heart kissed her lips gently and she felt his manhood grow against her the more they kissed. "My love," she climbed on top of him, she bit her bottom lip, and it turned him on like no other.

Wild Heart pulled her face down to kiss her again. "Never leave my side," she spread her legs so he could enter her. Mona let out a pleasing gasp and she started moving her hips slowly as he held onto her hips grinding into her. "Sweetheart, it has been so long," Wild Heart held her closer to him, so he could go deeper into her. It felt so good to them they could not hold out any longer, as they climaxed together and then fell asleep in a lovers embrace. They held on tightly to each other and slept like that for the rest of the night.

When Ruth had gotten up early the following morning, she headed to the dress shop; she was still baffled about last night and was not sure what to think about it, especially since Michael had taken her to bed and made love to her. "I love you, I love you!" kept playing repeatedly in her head. She was certain that in him speaking those words, he had cried, but did he mean it or was he thinking Mona? Ruth became worried and upset but there was not a thing she could do about it. She was his wife.

When Mona woke up, Wild Heart was sitting by her side holding their son Soaring Eagle; his smile was as bright as the sun. "He looks just like me!" Wild Heart's eyes were filled with joy and love. He leaned over and kissed her full lips, "No one has ever given me such a great gift, and I want more!" He placed his forehead against hers. Mona laughed, "Well then come back to bed," she said burying her face into his long flowing hair. Wild Heart took the sleeping baby and laid him in a bed that Eagle Eye had made for him and went back to bed to join his Rose.

When Michael got up he remembered last night, and it hurt his heart. He wondered to himself, "Did I call out Mona's name?" He was so scared and unsure and only Ruth could answer that question. Michael climbed out of bed and got dressed; to his surprise Ruth had already arrived home and was sporting a new dress. "She looks beautiful," he thought, but she wasn't Mona. "My love, maybe after last night I will bear you a son!" She walked over and kissed Michael on the lips. The only thing running through his head was that Mona gave another man a son and he should have been his son. Michael felt deep in his heart that he wanted Mona back so bad that he was willing to do anything to get her back, and that meant ANYTHING! Yet, Michael was not sure exactly where she was, but he was willing to search heaven and earth and bring her and THEIR son home by any means.

CHAPTER 8

Mona and Wild Heart stayed in until the evening, making love all through the morning. They enjoyed each other because they had missed so much time together; they were not ready to separate. They finally got up laughing and just enjoyed being together. "I have to get us something to eat so we will not perish in here together." Wild Heart chuckled at Mona, "Oh, I also have a surprise for you!" He laughed and kissed her full lips, she pulled him back into a lovers embrace. Finally releasing him from her lips and embrace, "Do you, well what is it?" she stood up as he was dressing. Wild Heart only smiled at her words. Mona grabbed him once again, pulled him into her soft silky skin, and locked onto his lips. Wild Heart kissed her back hard and gripped her soft, round bottom, Mona could feel his manhood rise once again, and she definitely liked that. Finally, Wild Heart broke free from her embrace, "That is why we shall die of hunger, cut it out," he laughed at her. Just then, Soaring Eagle began to cry, and Wild Heart took that as his out. He bent to kiss his son. She laughed lightly, "Oh how she loved this man."

Mona went and attended to the crying baby; she picked him up lovingly and soothed him. "You are a whiner just like your dad," she playfully giggled to the baby. Wild Heart pinched her bottom, "I shall be home soon." He kissed her as she held the baby and left.

After a while, Flower Fairy came to visit Mona and her grandson. She knew Mona would need help with the baby and she was more than happy to help her. "I have brought you something," she smiled handing Mona a beautiful dress. "What is this?" Mona beamed, "It is for your wedding daughter," as she hugged Mona. Excited, Mona could not contain her emotions "When?" She was so excited that she started to cry. Flower Fairy hugged her, "Your wedding will occur at the next full moon." Flower Fairy picked up her grandson and headed out to spend time with him.

At dinner, Michael tells his father that he is going away on a trip and that he needs a few men to go with him. "What exactly are looking for son?" Russell grins. "My property," Michael stated firmly. "Our property and I shall accompany you," Russell snarled. Ruth did not say a word; she just glared at Michael and he felt her glare up his spine. Ruth had thought they had gotten past this. They were going to enjoy their lives together, but he couldn't seem to get this bitch out of his system.

At the village, traders arrived to sell their wares. The people were familiar with them and since they do business there, they are welcomed and treated as brothers. Mona is unaware of the new visitors, but she heads out looking for Wild Heart. He hadn't returned home yet, and it was getting late. Flower Fairy and Eagle Eye still had Soaring Eagle, so she was bored. Mona noticed the traders and she got an uneasy feeling. The first one that she sees is tall and very handsome; the other was short and stocky. These men where very fit; another black man emerged carrying supplies. Mona was surprised that the black man was strikingly handsome, even more than the two men were, he was accompanying. The black man is followed up by yet, another white man and Mona gets very nervous, but she doesn't want to draw any attention to herself by running. Mona knew she had to avoid these men at all cost, she felt trouble in her gut, and she didn't like the feeling. Yet, she cannot help but to feel sympathy for this black man who is more than likely a slave.

Mona kept her head down trying to scurry past the men and not make eye contact. Out of nowhere, someone grabs Mona from behind and pulls her with such force. "Well, well, well what do we have here boys?" The man has a devilish grin. "She doesn't speak eh? I am Joseph, this is Bud and Bill." Mona's eyes dart to the handsome slave, "And that is John." he laughed. Mona tries to pull away from the men, "I must get going!" They block her path, "We are not good enough for you?" Joseph pulled her inches away from his face. Mona gets mad and very loud, "Take your hands off of me!" She yanked away from the men as hard as she could. The men all laughed, "Maybe John will be good enough for you," Bud chuckles to the other men. Joseph leans in to kiss her full lips, "You will take your hands off of her!" A deep thunderous voice bellowed; Wild Heart steps up and the men release her; Mona runs to Wild Heart and hides behind him. "Ah come on, we were only playing with her. I was unaware that Indians kept slaves," Joseph stated being nosey. "Black Rose is no slave and you will leave her be!" Wild Heart said forcefully. He was mad and he did not like seeing another man touch her. The thought of another's lips upon hers sent his blood boiling; he knew that if he had succeeded in kissing Mona, he would have killed the man. Wild Heart glared at the men, turned his back, picked Black Rose up, and carried her away from the men. Once they got back home, Wild Heart was furious and he started to yell at her. "What were you doing out there?" Mad that he was yelling at her she yelled back "I was looking for you" she snapped back. Wild Heart was mad and started to pace the floor. "A woman does not go around looking for a man." he pushed her. "You asshole!" she slapped his face, "I can't believe you would get so mad at me over this, how was I to know who was out there!" she screamed at him. Mona got so mad that he was being stubborn, so she said the meanest thing she could to him. "And you wonder why no one loves you?" she was pleased at her comment feeling that she had won the fight between them so she followed up with more harsh words to make it sting, "I might as well be with Michael!" With that, she sat down feeling vindicated. Wild Heart walked over to her mad and hurt; he glared at her and slapped her face, "Leave then!" Wild Heart left her there with a swollen cheeks and tears streaming down her face.

Mona was so mad and hurt and after cleaning her tears, she headed out to get her son. She came back home with Soaring Eagle and Wild Heart was still not back yet, so she decided not to stay any longer. Wild Heart told her to leave and so she shall get back to her original journey north. She would not allow her son to be taken into slavery. Mona laid down with the baby for a while; Wild Heart never came back so she gathered their things and headed off into the night with her son.

The next morning, Michael and Russell wait for the men to load up the supplies and the horses so they can head off to find Mona, both men were determined to have her at all cost. Ruth stayed inside the house; she wanted no part of this and she was not happy with them, so she refused to see them off. The men could care less; their sights were focused on finding Mona and nothing else. The men happily headed out with hopes of finding Mona, the sooner the better. Little did they know that Mona's mother, Dawn, had been hiding behind a tree watching and listening to the men. "Dear Lord, please watch over my baby and let them men leave her be." She sobbed for her daughter and hoped for the best. The men took off in a flash without looking back.

Wild Heart got up first thing the next morning to apologize to Black Rose and he noticed that she was gone. He stormed out and headed to the traders in the village, "Where is Black Rose?" Joseph stood to meet him, "We don't know where she is," he smiled. Wild Heart was certain they knew, so he punches him in the face and they start fighting. Chief Long Wind emerged and said, "Stop this now!" and the men scramble to their feet. "Maybe she has left on her own, leave it alone," Chief Long Wind states. "She would never leave me!" Wild Heart was furious. Just then, Blue Star walked up, "Oh, your slave finally ran away?" she laughed hysterically. Wild Heart gets in her face, "If you had anything to do with this, I will kill you," he yelled at her. Flower Fairy ran up to let him know that his son is gone too. Wild Heart is devastated, and he knows that this is beyond bad. Blue Star laughed all the way to the pond at Wild Heart's dismay, she spotted Mona and the baby walking towards her. "What are you doing here?" Blue Star snarls, "I am going home," Mona smiled; she did not get far as she could not bear to leave her love and she felt that they both were just scared and had overreacted. She wanted to make it up to him and apologize. "You do realize that Wild Heart was with me last night, right?" Blue Star smirks in Mona's face, "He would never!" Mona snapped back. "He told me of your fight and came to me for comfort. He no longer loves you, and is now willing to marry me." Blue Star looks Mona up and down, "He has asked the traders to take you away and I will raise your son as my own." She put her arms out to take the baby from Mona. "No, he is my son!" Mona backed away, "You may have Wild Heart, but you will not get my son!" holding the baby against her chest. "Fine, do you want me to help you then, so you can keep him with you?" she looked at Mona in disgust. "Please," Mona started to cry, she didn't think their fight had warranted such harshness. "Wait here, but hide and I will get you a horse" Blue Star walked off pleased at the damage she has caused. Nevertheless, she would soothe Wild Heart and heal his heart.

Blue Starr paid a visit to the traders in the village, "You know that the slave girl he pines for is a runaway slave and worth a lot of money?" she smiled; "They will pay any ransom to get her back, she is very valuable" Blue Star smiled devilishly. "What's in it for you?" Joseph asked "Wild Heart," she laughed and then told the traders Mona's whereabouts and they left the tribe to go seek her out. Eagle Eye noticed the conversation and he did not like their interaction one bit; the traders headed out to the pond and found Black Rose, "My dear Mona, we meet again" Joseph grabbed a hold of her face and kissed her full lips as Mona bit him hard and pulled back. "My husband will kill you!" she screamed as she held her fear in, the man laughed, "Blue Star will make sure that he forgets you!" They give the baby to John and load Mona into the wagon. The men mount their horses and John held the baby as security, so she did not try to escape.

Michael and Russell were not doing so well, Russell was severely ill and getting worse; the men must turn back around to go home and see a doctor. "Son, I am fine" Russell started throwing up blood. "We will wait a few days and then head back out again," Michael tells his father as he wipes his face.

Wild Heart sits in his tepee very angry and upset as Blue Star walked in, "I will help you through this," she puts her hand in his hair and rubs his head. "Leave me be," Wild Heart grabbed her hand. "I will go but I will be around when you need me" Blue Star smiled and left.

Mona was devastated and could not stop crying. "Hush now sweet girl, there is nothing us slaves can do, at least you got a taste of freedom," John tried to comfort her. "Don't you want that too?" she asked him with tear-filled eyes. "Quiet down now before they hear you," John shushed her. "Let's run John!" "We cannot with the baby" John sighed. Mona proceeded to cry her eyes out for Wild Heart, "Where was he?" Why was he not looking for her? She knew he couldn't have meant what he said during their fight; she was mad at herself for listening to Blue Star. Mona was at a loss, she did not know what to do or think. John tried to talk to Mona once again and to help ease her pain.

CHAPTER 9

Wild Heart was sitting inside of his tepee angry as fire when Eagle Eye came in to tell him about what he had seen with Blue Star and the traders. Wild Heart thought back to their fight, "She left because I hit her." Eagle Eye looked at his brother in surprise, "Why would you do such a thing?" "I was upset and jealous, the way they looked at her made me sick to my stomach. I don't want any man to ever touch her or look at her that way." Wild Heart felt his heart become extremely heavy, "I am afraid that she will find someone better and leave me!" Wild Heart could not contain his sadness in front of his brother. Eagle Eye went to his brother and hugged him "She chose you; she gave you her heart and a son." Wild Heart nodded. "Let's go out and find her before anything bad happens to her." Wild Heart and Eagle Eye left together to go find Black Rose and Soaring Eagle.

Mona was so terrified by now, "Where will they take her? What will they do with her son?" John tried his best to comfort her but there was no comfort in the unknown. It made her so much more upset and she missed Wild Heart like crazy.

After days of riding almost non-stop, Mona realized they were headed back to the Russell plantation. Mona was officially scared now, and she couldn't do anything about it. As they reached the front of the house, Mona's mother, Dawn, stepped out of the house and her eyes filled with tears; all she could do was cry for her baby girl. Michael walked around Dawn and stared down at Mona and all that crosses his mind was, "My wife has returned." "Welcome home Mona," he smiled at her slyly. Ruth stared out of the window and watched Michael make a fool out of himself. "How can I get rid of this bitch?" Ruth wondered. The traders pulled Mona down from the wagon and they handed Soaring Eagle back to her. Dawn stared at the small bundle in her daughters' arms. Love, joy, and sadness swept over her and she could only pray that this was not Michael's child. Because if it was, she knew her daughter would never be free again. Michael motioned Dawn to go to her daughter and her grandson. "Take her upstairs and lock her up!" Michael stated arrogantly, he turned to the traders, "Come let us discuss your rewards."

When they had gotten upstairs, Mona told her mother of her journeys. Dawn was excited because she had never been anywhere. Dawn had felt the pain of lost love just as her daughter had. She fell in love at a young age with her previous master's son who was a half-breed; his mother was native. He was the father of Mona and her younger sister Natalya. Dawn was told that he had been killed in battle when he joined the war, but her heart never had accepted this, she did not believe he was dead. Grey Storm was the son of a white plantation owner and his mother was Native American and black; she died when he was eight years old of pneumonia. Dawn had loved him as soon as they had met, Mona loved to hear the story of her parents, and she asked if she would tell her about it again.

(Flash Back)

Dawn was ten years old when she was sold from her parents to the "Stone plantation". She had worked in the house, cooking and cleaning. She was also a playmate to a small five-year-old girl named Lisa, the master's only daughter; they had been bonded for years and were together constantly. Dawn had never known that Master Stone had a son; when Mona was seventeen and Lisa was twelve they did everything together almost as if they were sisters. Dawn had gotten to the point where she barely worked in the house because Lisa requested her frequently.

Finally, Lisa had told Dawn that she had a brother that had just finished college and was on his way home. "I never knew you had a brother," Dawn smiled. "My father keeps him a secret because my mother hates him." Lisa frowned, "Now that he is grown he will become the heir to the Stone Plantation and my mother cannot stop it. "Why does your mother hate him?" Dawn was confused, "He is a half breed and my mother hated his mother, hurry let's go!" Lisa pulled Dawn into the train station, "He should be arriving any minute!" Lisa was excited and she loved her brother despite her mother's hatred. "Are you coming?" Lisa held out her hand to Dawn and she took it and they ran to stand on the train station platform. They waited patiently for Grey Storm to step off the train…

(Flash Back Ends)

A young man stepped off the train onto the platform, his hair was jet-black and fell into waves on his shoulders, and the sun beamed off his tan skin illuminating his grey eyes. He stood about 6-foot-tall with broad shoulders and his muscles ripples under his shirt. Dawn's mouth dropped at the sight of him. Lisa ran to him as he bent down with his arms wide open, "Hey Kiddo!" Grey Storm scooped Lisa up into his arms; he had missed his little sister dearly.

Dawn stood there in awe; she was petite with two long braids that fell past her shoulders. Dawn had an awkward disposition, but her smile was amazing with full dimples. She had a scar on her face that ran from her eye to her lips; she and Lisa had been playing when an accident caused Lisa to get hurt. However, Dawn was beat for it leaving her face marked. Dawn had big deep brown eyes and she stood at 5 foot 2 inches. Grey Storm took note of her big brown eyes that seemed to stare into his soul. He chuckled, "The must be Dawn, whom I have heard so much about," he took her hand and kissed it giving her his award-winning smile. "He has so much charm," Dawn thought as she felt her face flush. Dawn smiled and did a small curtsy. "What are you about 14?" Grey Storm teased, poking fun at the bashful girl. "I am almost 18," she finally mustered up her voice and he chuckled at her forced words. "It was cute that she was too flustered to talk coherently," he thought.

On the way back to the plantation, they had poked fun at one another and caught up on things that had been missed by the two siblings. That became the start of a beautiful friendship between Dawn and Grey Storm. From there on out and little by little they had become reliant on each other. That following year, Grey Storm had confessed his love for her and shortly after Mona was born. Dawn and Grey Storm had loved each other so deeply and neither could hide it; he protected her, his daughter, and the unborn child in her belly. Grey Storm had to leave before Natalya was born but he promised his love that he would return, but he never did. Deep in her heart, Dawn had felt that Grey Storm was sent away on purpose because others were jealous of their relationship. Lisa did not approve of the couple and Dawn felt he had been sent far away and never to return, so he would forget about her and their family.

Mona always cried at the story of her parents and her absent father; this made her more determined than anything to find her way back to Wild Heart even if it killed her, she had to see him again.

Dawn had told her daughter that she had planned on an escape to find her father and now that the girls were grown, she yearned even more for her lost love. Lisa had agreed to meet with Dawn, so they could talk and catch up; Dawn and the girls had been sold almost immediately and which was why Dawn had always felt something was amiss. Mona asked her mother about her sister Natalya, "She was very upset that you had left without her." Dawn stroked Mona's head "Mama! She wasn't ready!" Mona moaned. Dawn grabbed Mona by the face looking deep into her eyes "She's ready now baby, do not leave her here to suffer! You hear me?" Dawn held a stern face. "Mama!" Mona started to whine again, "Don't worry about me; I'm going to find your daddy or die trying!" Dawn kissed her grandson and left.

Wild Heart and Eagle Eye were trying to figure out where Rose might be, "I bet she is back at her home on the plantation!" Wild Heart shook his head. Eagle Eye turned to his brother "Blue Star is following" he whispered, "Good; we will use her as a trade and let her become the slave." Wild Heart kicked his horse to go faster so he could set a trap for her.

When the next morning came, Mona's back had become extremely stiff and sore from the long ride. Michael had sent in some of the slaves to care for Mona and the baby. Mona was not sure what to make of why he was being so nice to her. Michael had gotten up early and went into town to get things for her and the baby, but he never came in personally to deliver the items or speak to her. He even sent in her sister, Natalya, late the night before to stay in her room with them. "What is he up to Natalya?" Mona was beyond confused, "I do not know and I'm scared too!" Natalya was serious.

Natalya was 21 and more beautiful than her big sister was; she took after her father. She had honey colored eyes and soft olive tanned skin. She had huge dimples in her cheeks and her hair was a curly brownish red that fell to the middle of her back. Natalya had never thought anyone was ever good enough for her and no one liked her, except for her sister; she had the reputation of a bully. Natalya's best friend was Dennis and they would go to town and bully and play tricks on others, as well as each other. Natalya had been raised with more freedom than anyone had because of her looks had, but Dennis always reminded her how ugly and gross she looked.

"Do not leave me behind this time!" She yelled at Mona. "I will not stay and die here alone, do you hear me?" She laid her head on her sister's lap.

CHAPTER 10

Wild Heart began setting up a trap for Blue Star, while Eagle Eye wandered off to hide on a nearby path, so when she passed by he could grab her. Wild Heart went to a nearby creek to get a drink and eat his jerky; Blue Starr could not help but to try to move closer to him. Out of nowhere, Eagle Eye jumped her from behind and grabbed her, Blue Star screamed for help because she couldn't see who was jumping her from behind. Eagle Eye spent her around so fast it knocked her onto the ground. Wild Heart rushed up, and both warriors gasp when they notice her belly is swollen.

"You're having a baby?' Wild Heart said in a shocking manner; Blue Star cried, "Yes! Shut up! I am following you to get to the father and see if he will accept me and his child." Blue Star was trying to hold back her emotions. Eagle Eye laughed riotously "She probably doesn't even know who the father is!" He picked her up. "I do so know!" Now she was mad, she fully stood to face Wild Heart. Wild Heart placed her hands together; "If she wants to go we will gladly take her," Eagle Eye tied her hands." He threw his brother the rope.

Later, an intoxicated Michael creeped in to see Mona; she had fallen asleep with the baby in her arms. He stood over her and watched her sleep. Mona woke up almost instantly, "That should be my son!" Michael looked at Mona with unblinking anger on his face. "There is no way Michael!" Mona sat up and laid the sleeping baby down. He became agitated and sad, "But, you told me that you loved me." He sat on the foot of her bed and tears started to swell up in his eyes, they forced their way out and rolled down his red puffy cheeks. "Michael, I do... Well I did but I knew that it could never be; my heart has moved on to another and I love him dearly." Mona stroked the sleeping baby's face. All emotion suddenly left Michael's face, "You are here now, and if that Indian comes for you and my son. I will KILL him." He stood up with all his pain and rage showing on his face; Mona knew that he had meant every word he had said. Mona stood to face him, "He is not your son!" She was afraid of him at that moment, but she would not show it. "If I say he is, then he IS my son, and no one can challenge that!" Michael stormed out of the room.

Michael ran into Ruth in the hallway as he stormed out of Mona's room. "He is NOT your son and we are selling them separately!" Ruth slapped Michael's face with all her might; she was hurt and mad. Michael slapped her back just as hard "You will go first!" Ruth was stunned; he turned to walk away but then grabbed her and pulled her along "Let's go to bed now." Michael dragged her back to the bedroom.

The next morning Michael realized just how drunk he had been last night, and all that he had done and said. He rolled over in bed to face his wife, "I am sorry!" She pretended to be asleep; she had already been up for a while. She had been deep in thought, trying to figure out her next move. Ruth rolled over pretending that she was still sleep. She was still thinking about ways to get rid of Mona; she silently vowed to herself that even if she had to go behind Michael's back, she would sell Mona and that bastard son she loved so much.

Mona woke up and her sister had already came over and tended to the baby. Natalya loved him so much and couldn't wait to have one of her own. "We have been here for months and after last night I know the time to run again is now," She confided in her little sister. Natalya placed her hand on her sister's forehead, "You feel warm and you look flushed and tired," Mona whispered to her sister "I am pregnant, but please don't tell a soul," She held her sisters arm tightly.

Dawn came to see the girls and her grandson "I finally got to visit with Lisa today." She smiled at the girls. "And?" they say simultaneously as they moved closer in to hear their mother's words. Dawn caught her breath, "You're pregnant!" Looking Mona dead in the face, she said, "I know mom, be quiet; no one knows yet and I don't want them knowing either." Mona moved swiftly towards the door to make sure no one was eavesdropping. "So, how did it go mom?" Natalya grabbed her mother's hand. "Your father is still alive!" Dawn's face was beaming with joy and tears fell from her face.

Wild Heart was getting angry, "This trip is taking way too long!" "Because we got lost a few times, bad weather, and let's not forget I am pregnant you twit!" Blue Star yelled at him. Eagle

Eye laughed, "Her hormones are all over the place, and you two need to calm down." "Don't make us leave you!" Eagle Eye was fed up with Blue Star; after all she had done he wouldn't mind leaving her behind to suffer and die but the unborn child in her stomach was saving her life right now. "Let's go" Wild Heart yelled, "We have stopped long enough; we need to go now." The warriors loaded the horses back up to head out once again.

Ruth came in to see Mona and asked if she could see the baby, but Mona didn't trust Ruth. "Why do you need to see him?" Mona got in front of Soaring Eagle while he sat on the floor playing. "I want to take him to the market." Ruth's voice became very stern as she started to reach for the child. " NO! Natalya stood up, "You will not touch him!" attempting to protect her sister and nephew. Ruth laughed, "You have never cared about anyone other than yourself!" Ruth took a step forward. "I have grown up!" Natalya got in front of her sister and the child. Ruth hit Natalya with a closed fit causing her to hit the bedpost while she fell to the ground, Natalya had blood rushing down her face. "Give the little bastard to me now!" She screamed at Mona, snatching Soaring Eagle away; he started to cry and screamed for his mother. Just then, the overseer comes in and places Mona in shackles and they dragged her back out to the slave quarters, and no one was to remove her shackles.

Mona wailed all day and by that night, she was still up in a state of shock and devastation. Michael heard about what had happened and he rushed to see Mona once he returned late last night. Mona was in shackles on the bed and she didn't even lift her head to look up at him. "I have been looking for you, I just got home!" Michael moved closer to her, "I came to apologize to you about the other night." He kneeled down by her side but she didn't look up or make a sound. Michael grabbed her face and her eyes were bloody, and red "You should apologize for stealing my son!" Monas gaze became icy "I promise that if you do not return my son, your family will all die!" Mona had lost her mind, but she meant what she had said to him. One single tear escaped her eye, as she had no more tears left. Michael pulled her face to his, "Who has taken your son?" Michael looked confused because he had not heard about this part of the story. "Your wife did this to me!" Mona had just enough strength left so she slapped his face; she no longer cared about the consequences. "I didn't know anything about this and I will get him back for you." Michael started to cry, and he hugged Mona tightly. "I have done you wrong in every way, but in this, I will do right by you." He got to his feet and apologized softly to her "I'm sorry," he starts to leave. "Michael!" Mona yelled to him and he turned back to face her "Just let us leave peacefully, I beg you," Mona had hope in her eyes but Michael just turned and left. The sight of her like a caged animal had broken his soul, all he wanted to do was love her and keep her safe, and he is starting to realize it is impossible for him to do either without causing her more strife.

A few weeks passed by and there was still no word. Finally one morning Ruth came in holding Soaring Eagle, "Here is your son" she handed him to Mona. Mona looked up to see that Ruth had bruises on her face and arms, Michael walked in "Now Leave!" he demanded of Ruth and she walked out obediently with her head down. Mona hugged Soaring Eagle tightly kissing his cheeks and making sure, he was ok. "Where did you find him?" Mona asked Michael and he puts his head down. "She had sold him," he was very ashamed. Mona stood up to face him "When can we leave?" she asked him. "I do not know if I am willing to do that, I still love you very much." He said as he sat by her.

Mona clutched her son hiding her belly and starts to cry, she knows that she has to do something. Her belly is getting bigger and who knows how he will react to the news she has been hiding from him. "I can't stop loving you; I have always wanted you by my side." Michael grabbed her arm with one hand and stroked her cheek with his other. "Michael, I belong to another man!" She pulled away from him. "Michael, you have to understand that we both need to accept what cannot and will not ever be!" Mona touched his hand. "No one can take away what we felt for each other, nor our deep bond." She faced him trying to convince him to release her. "Listen, keeping me against my will, will never make me love you anymore nor, will our bond be spared." "Michael, you need to realize that it is over between us but we can stay friends."

Michael's eyes swelled up, he knew that she was right and no matter what, nothing could change. "This is all my fault and I don't know if I have the strength to let you go." He laid his head in her lap, "Life will not be the same without you Mona." Mona wiped his tears, "You have lived for years with only a memory of me, so why can't you do it now?" Mona lifted his head up, "Should I be made to suffer more at your father's hand and have my child sold when your wife tires of us?" Mona placed her forehead against his, "Please Michael with all the love you hold for me, release me." Michael lifted his head "My father... you are right, my father will do all he can to hurt you. I will let you go, but I need you to know that I love you and I will take part of a way to protect you." He kissed her lips and she allowed it as long as she was able to leave. She grabbed his arm once their lips parted, "Michael I need my sister; please release Natalya and I will find someone to take her place." Michael gave a half smile, "I will allow it." Mona was happy, and she knew just who would take her sister's spot; she was certain that they were already on their way to her.

Wild Heart was getting frustrated, "I will not give up on finding my Rose; she has never given up on me!" Eagle Eye hoped and prayed for his brother; he knew how he felt about Black Rose. Eagle Eye also wished that he had someone to feel that way about. Blue Star complained the whole way and it took everything in Wild Heart's power not to strike her off her horse. He knew that all of this was her doing and he would make her pay for the pain that she caused him and his family.

Natalya and Dawn came in to see Soaring Eagle, "How is everything Mona?" her mother hugged her. "Mom, Michael is taking us part of the way back and Natalya too," Mona was happy, she hadn't smiled this much in months. "I'm happy for you baby, I am leaving myself to go find your father, and when all is said and done, I will come find you two at your new home!" She hugged and kissed her girls. "Wait, mom what if dad has another family? What if he doesn't care about us anymore?" Dawn patted her back, "Hush now child that is for me to worry about." Mona finished gathering up the baby's things while her mother played with him. " Watch Mona," her mom called out and Soaring Eagle stood up and took a few steps. Mona can't help but cry, "I wish Wild Heart was here to see this" Dawn hugged her daughter. "Tell me about him child," her mother comforted her. 'Mom, I actually met him while saving his life. I had never dreamed that I could love another man nor that anyone could love me that much! Mama, you would love him so!" Mona's face lit up with joy when she spoke of her love.

Natalya finally returned, as it was getting dark. Michael showed up shortly after, "Are you both ready to go?" he strolled towards Mona, "Yes, what about your father?" she looked into his eyes. "As far as I know, he is not even been informed that you are here. His health had been bad, but he was slowly getting better and any day now he will be back to his old self." Michael motioned them to go out the door. They grab everything and head out the door, but little did they know Ruth had been there listening to every word Michael had said. She vowed that she would pay Mona back for stealing away his love, causing Michael to have her beaten.

They headed towards the stable where Michael had a wagon waiting for them. Mona climbed in and Michael hands Soaring Eagle to her; he paused and looked at the child, "He is such a beautiful child, he looks like you." Mona grabbed him, "Thank you Michael" They smile at each other. "I hope that one day Ruth will tell me that she is with child," he smiled helping Natalya into the wagon. Dawn stood back waving goodbye to her daughters and grandson, "I promise to join you girls and if not, do not worry, wherever I am, I am blessed and happy!" she wiped tears from her eyes. "Dawn, I have been to this place, I will take you there to visit." He hugged the girl's mom and climbed on the front of the wagon with the driver and Dennis.

Time has passed, and they had been driving for; the girls were asleep. "Michael, if you loved her and wanted her back so badly, why did you let her leave?" Dennis asked cautiously. "I love her too much to force her to be with me and she was right, we've made it this long on just the hope of each other." he sighed "I don't want to lose my best friend, if it is meant to be, we will find our way back to each other." Dennis nodded to his big brother, "That is a good decision."

As early morning approached, Mona was awakened by Soaring Eagle babbling, "Da da" and slobbering on her face. "Good morning my little warrior," she kissed his fat cheeks. The wagon came to a halt, and they spotted several riders approaching. Michael spoke with the white men and then they continued on their way. They traveled a little further, and decided to rest in midafternoon near a pond. Michael and Dennis make a pallet near the wagon along with the driver to sleep. Mona laid Soaring Eagle down, she thought; "I will find us some food for when the men woke up and Natalya decided to go take a dip in the pond.

They did not know that Eagle Eye was near the pond as well; Eagle Eye went up to the pond and suddenly stopped in his tracks.

CHAPTER 11

Never has he seen a woman so beautiful in his life. The woman didn't notice that she was being watched. Finally, Natalya emerged from the water and slowly turned and caught Eagle Eye watching. Devastated, she screamed out, "HELP!" Wild Heart came running to see what all the commotion was about and he started laughing as Natalya fell back into the water while trying to get dressed quickly. Wild Heart laughed hysterically "Wait!" Eagle Eye yelled to the woman but she ran off. Natalya stopped in her tracks and Eagle Eye walked over to her, she turned her back to him "That was very rude of you to watch me," she snapped at him, "I am so sorry beautiful one," he held out his hand to her. Natalya was impressed by how handsome he was, "If my sister thinks Indians are so great, maybe I'll try this out," she thought.

"Are you spoken for?" Eagle Eye asked her with curious eyes, "No, I am not." Natalya blushed but just then, Natalya heard Soaring Eagle cry out. "Soaring Eagle, I must get to him!" she ran off towards the wagon. Eagle Eye snapped back to reality, "Did you just say Soaring Eagle?" Natalya kept going so Eagle

Eye called for Wild Heart and Blue Star and they all followed Natalya.

Natalya reached for Soaring Eagle and picked him up, as Mona was not back yet, Wild Heart rushed at Natalya and took the crying child. "This is my son!" he yelled at her. Michael and Dennis rose to their feet. Eagle Eye glared at Natalya, "What are you doing with these men and my nephew?" he grabbed her, "He is my nephew as well," she yanked loose from his grasp and ran over to Wild Heart taking Soaring Eagle back. Soaring Eagle reached for Wild Heart, "da da," Natalya handed him back to Wild Heart. Just then, Mona returned, and she stopped in her tracks at the sight of her love. Michael ran over to Mona, she had a look of tremendous pain on her face. "Are you alright darling?" Michael placed his hand upon her back, Wild Heart rushed over. " Take your hands off my wife!" with that, he pushed Michael back. Blue Star finally caught up and headed to Dennis, "I have been looking for you," as she held her swollen belly. Dennis laughed hysterically, "It's not mine!" Blue Star slapped him across the face, "You will take care of us." Natalya stepped forward, "Michael, there is your trade for my freedom, keep her" she smiled at Blue Star.

Dennis loaded Blue Star onto the wagon. Wild Heart gave Soaring Eagle to Natalya and picked up Mona. "Are you alright my love?" Sweat was dropping from her forehead and the pain was beyond anything she has ever felt, and she couldn't hide this any longer, "I am pregnant!" Mona started to cry, and Wild Heart was so happy that he started to sing. Eagle Eye walked up to Natalya and took Soaring Eagle from her "What are you doing?"

Natalya snapped "Holding my favorite nephew," he smiled at her coyly. Natalya can't help but to smile at him; there is something so attractive about Eagle Eye, she must get closer to him.

"We need to leave as soon as possible, she needs medical attention." Wild Heart placed Mona on the wagon. Mona started bleeding "It's too soon for the little one to come out," Mona cried. "You'll be fine; there is a farm just a little way up the road" Michael gestured to her. "NO! I do not want your help," Wild Heart yelled at him. "Our baby may die, please leave him be" Mona grabbed Wild Heart's hand. "Fine, but only for you." Wild Heart kissed her sweat soaked forehead. They get up to leave and Wild Heart looks at Mona, "ride with me," he reached a hand out; he did not want to chance losing her again. Natalya stepped in between them, "She needs to ride in the wagon and lay down, you can get in with her, and I will ride your horse." She grabbed the reigns. Wild Heart jumped down and got in the wagon with her and Eagle Eye helped Natalya onto her horse.

After a while, they finally come up on a small farm. Michael goes in and talks to the owners. The woman is home alone with her small daughter while her husband is away. The woman agreed to only let Mona in for now and Soaring Eagle if need be. Wild Heart did not like this arrangement, but he agreed, so he would He would not let his son out of his sight; he refused to lose them both.

Meanwhile, Ruth was helping to nurse Russell back to health. Ruth told Russell how Michael and Dennis had Mona but then took her back, Russell was livid. Russell decided that once he is better, he will go after them, and he tried to convince Ruth that she should leave Michael, she would not accept his nonsense because he was not a man. Russell just decided to make the trip anyway and have the men load up the wagon and Ruth told him, "I am going with you!" Russell laughed, "Be ready by dawn," he went back to bed.

While Mona was being tended to and Wild Heart had taken the baby. Natalya and Eagle Eye started spending a lot of time together while they wait and see how Mona is doing. "Your brother seems to love my sister a lot, I hope one day to find such a love." She smiled, and Eagle Eye cannot help it; he is so overwhelmed by her beauty, he grabbed her and kissed her softly. Natalya had first resisted his kiss but then she snuggled herself into his arms. Natalya had never really much been into men, her main goal was to leave the plantation, and she had done just that. She could not believe how much he had made her want more. Eagle Eye led Natalya to the barn and they laid it in the soft hay. They kissed and enjoyed each other's company. "I am saving myself for my husband," She made sure he was fully aware of her intentions, "And I shall be him." Eagle Eye kissed her, "And I shall wait a lifetime for you," she giggled and snuggled into him. Wild Heart walked in holding Soaring Eagle, "I must see my Rose; it had been two days, "Please watch him." he handed the baby to Eagle Eye and Natalya. Wild Heart turned to leave but then turned back to them, "Are you two…?" he stopped his sentence laughed, shook his head and left. Michael saw Wild Heart heading to the house and ran up, "I'm coming with you." Wild Heart stopped in his tracks, "That is my wife and child in there, not yours! Moreover, why are you even still here? This is your fault, leave my family alone!" He huffed and walked on.

"You are right, I should leave! Can I at least say goodbye to her?" Michael demanded. "Fine," Wild Heart continued to the house and knocked on the door. The woman opened the door quickly and motioned for him to come in. "Its time!" She belted out and ran back over to Mona. Wild Heart runs in behind the woman where Mona is screaming and crying in pain. The baby is coming too early and I cannot stop it, Wild Heart kissed her forehead, "Baby I am sorry, it will be fine, I am here" he grabbed ahold of her hand. At that exact moment, Michael, for the first time realized that the love they shared was unique and no one else can break it or come between them. The love that Michael had for Mona would never amount to what Wild Heart had for her. A single tear fell from his eyes, he fell instantly to his knees crying, and Wild Heart looked over at him confused. "I am so sorry for all the hurt I have caused you," Michael crawled to the side of the bed. "I now understand your love and I have done unspeakable things; please forgive me, I will never bother you again!" He stood upright, "Maybe one day I will share in such a love," he walked out and got Dennis and Blue Star, and so they can all head home.

Mona is still in agony hardly hearing what Michael said but Wild Heart heard him and nodded. The woman was trying to make sure that everything was all right while Wild Heart was trying to calm Mona down; Mona lets out a painful cry and Wild Heart watches in pain as blood rushes from between her legs and out pops a little head! Wild Heart had never seen such a sight and normally men were not allowed to be around during birthing, but he had no choice, he was needed. The woman helped assist the baby out and once she was free and clear the woman handed Wild Heart the baby, "It's a girl," she said smiling but Mona was still yelling in pain. The woman went back down and gasped at the sight she sees "Oh my Goodness," she shouted and Wild Heart jumped to his feet and let Mona's hand go to see what was wrong. "Another one?" He cried with joy; baby we have two girls!" Wild Heart jumped up and down, the great gods had given him a double blessing.

Mona is so tired that she barely hears a thing, "Oh no, she's losing a lot of blood." The woman ran out of the house to get the doctor, while Wild Heart stayed with Mona and the girls. After a while, the woman came back in with the doctor. Mona had already stopped bleeding, Wild Heart was tending to her, and she fell asleep. The doctor had given her a shot to soothe the pain, so she could sleep longer; he checked on the girls making sure they were healthy; the smaller one seemed to be having a little trouble breathing so the doctor said to keep an eye on her and he told Wild Heart that they should all be fine.

A knock at the door brought him back to reality; it was Natalya, Eagle Eye, and Soaring Eagle, "Is everything alright?" they asked. Wild Heart quickly gathered up the two small bundles and approached them; "My two daughters meet your big brother," he smiled with pride. "Two girls!" Eagle Eye was more overwhelmed with joy, "How did this happen?" he was stunned and thankful that his brother was so blessed. The pair cooed over the babies then returned to the barn to get some rest. The woman let Wild

Heart stay to help with the babies while Soaring Eagle stayed with Natalya and Eagle Eye.

The morning was chilly, and Ruth could not wait to get even with Michael and Mona. Everything was loaded up; everyone was waiting on Russell and he was still not feeling at his best, but he was determined to make the trip. Russell hobbled out of the house still very sick; he seemed worse than the previous day but ignored any other thoughts on the matter. "Where is my horse?" He coughed up phlegm. They brought out his horse and saddled it up for him. Russell had to be assisted in mounting his horse; he looked terrible but if anyone said anything about it, that person would be severely punished. Everyone set off and rode in complete silence.

Eagle Eye grabbed a blanket, laid down next to Natalya, and snuggled up to her. "The great Gods sent you to me," He kissed her forehead, "You are so sweet, how is it that no one has taken you already?" She giggled at him. "I was waiting for you," he hugged her tightly. "Please do not be a dream," he pinched her, and they laughed.

After a couple of days of riding slow because they continuously stopped because Russell was getting weaker and weaker, yet no one could speak about it. The men started to wonder if he would even survive the trip long enough to make it. Hardly making progress, they got lucky and ran into Michael and Dennis. "Father, what are you doing here and out of bed?" Michael's eyes shot to Ruth. "Dad you look awful," Dennis chimed in. Russell started to cough "Ask your wife, son," Russell let out a wheezed snicker. Michael glared at Ruth. He was beyond angry,

"Father it is over, let's turn back and go home!" Michael did not break his glare from Ruth. Dennis was not too fond of Ruth either and he knew his brother was pissed; hell, he was too.

I'll handle you when we get back home!" Michael finally broke off his glare from Ruth. Ruth had become nervous and felt a bit uneasy, but then she shrugged it off as it meant nothing to her and she just smiled back at him. Blue Star appeared from the wagon and stared Ruth down. Now Ruth became scared of what the Indian girl might do to her; Blue Star leaned back into the wagon but stayed watching Ruth. The boys tended to their father. "This is done, we will leave here in the morning, he needs rest," Michael tells the group.

Dennis approached Ruth, "If he dies because of this wasted trip, you will pay dearly," he yelled, Blue Star stared in the background and nodded in agreement. Ruth knew they were truly serious and would cause her great harm if she didn't plan accordingly.

It was getting dark outside and Mona started to stir, "Perfect timing, the girls are hungry." Wild Heart leaned in and kissed her forehead. "I have never loved you as much as I do right now at this very moment," he said with soft eyes as he kissed her full lips. "I love you" she tried to speak; Wild Heart ran to get her some water, she drank it up hungrily and he ran back to get her some more water. "My darling," Mona placed her hand softly on his cheek. "I have no idea what to name our girls," Wild Heart laughed, "We will know what is in our hearts to name them, and I promise you they shall have great names," he stroked her cheek. Wild Heart went and got the girls and brought them to Mona so she could feed them; the girls suckled until they fell asleep feeding and Wild Heart went and laid them back down.

Wild Heart climbed into bed with Mona, she snuggled up to him, and fell asleep in his warm embrace. He watched her sleep; she looked so peaceful and his eyes swelled up thinking "How could one person love another person so much?" He loved her with every bit of his heart and his soul. Mona woke to Wild Heart rubbing her face, as her eyes fluttered open he kissed her soft lips, "My Rose, how are you feeling?" He held onto her hand and kissed it. Wild Heart once again went to get the girls and bring them to Mona for feeding, "So, have you figured out what to name them yet?" Mona teased him. Wild Heart stared in shock, "Me?" Mona kissed his hand, "Yes, you." She kissed him holding onto his bottom lip a bit longer. Wild Heart paused as he thought, "How about Luyu and Ogin?" Mona stared in confusion and he laughed at her. "They mean, Wild Dove (Luyu), and Wild Rose (Ogin)." He looked at her, "Oh," and she smiled. "I love them, now I have my own Wild Dove and Wild Rose," she nodded in agreement.

Eagle Eye and Natalya came to speak to Wild Heart. "Brother, we have been here too long; we need to make it back home very soon." Wild Heart knew that his brother was right, "Prepare the wagon and we shall leave at dawn," he leaned down to kiss Mona on the forehead "Are you able to make the trip home my love?" Mona kissed him deeply, "I will follow you anywhere," she sat up.

The next morning, they loaded the wagon for the journey home and Mona thanked the woman for everything and bid her and the small child farewell. Mona laid in the wagon with the babies to rest; her body was still tired from all she had been through and then such a painful childbirth. The journey will take them awhile, but they knew that they had to leave and get Mona back safely so she can finish recovering. They took such great care in watching the twins. Mona and Wild Heart watched them sleep and he silently vowed his complete loyalty to them. He knew that Mona was his soul mate and he would never love another like he loved her, and he would never leave her side; she had given him what no other woman ever could. "Wholeness." Wild Heart wanted to do something sweet for her once she was up and well, and back to her old self. He knew that she deserved the world and she had already been through way too much; never again would he let her go.

As Michael rode home next to Ruth, he knew what he had to do. It took everything in him not to reach over and choke her to death. Mostly, he stayed silently angry unless he had to speak with his brother, his only true support system. Michael wondered how it would go over once he made the announcement to leave Ruth.

Ruth was a rotten apple from the inside out he knew that she loved him dearly, but he loved Mona more and if she was going to be a threat to her, he didn't want her in his life. The ride seemed to last forever to Michael and to Ruth the silence was killing her. She did not feel that she had gotten her point across to Michael, but she vowed that she would make him understand. No matter the cost, if he did not willingly love her then she would force his love. Ruth tried to reach over and touch Michael, but he led his horse away and he would not allow it, it was getting late, so she spoke up, "I'm tired and daddy looks famished, let's eat and make camp for the night," she smiled slyly. "Sounds good to me," Russell groaned and Ruth smiled devilishly, they had fallen right into her plans. As they set up to eat, Ruth devised a plan to finally get rid of Mona so she could have all of Michael's love to herself.

CHAPTER 12

Once they arrived home, Russell was taken to his room and the doctor was called in to check on his condition. "You were in no condition for traveling, what is wrong with you?" The doctor stated forcefully. "I warned you two before you left here, that it could be fatal to your health and just look at you now!" The doctor glared at Ruth as she put her head down. "I know Doc, but there was something that I had to tend to; it needed my utmost attention and could not wait! I'm sorry," Russell started to cough up blood. Russell was getting worse by the minute and the doctor made everyone leave his room so he could give him a full check over and medicate him so that he could get some well-needed rest. The doctor was very unhappy with the situation, he had spoken to Ruth previously, and she knew the consequences of her actions.

Michael went to his study, he needed a quiet place because his mind and emotions were running wild and he felt he needed some control and a stiff drink. Ruth waited until he was good and settled in his study before she followed him in; she was willing to chance whatever he was going to say or do to her. When Ruth crept into the study Michael was sitting in his chair glaring at the fire; he was slouched and his head hung down; she was unsure if he was in a daze or half asleep. Without making any movement, "Why did you do this?" His voice was monotone and unfeeling. "What do you mean?" she asked trying to pretend that she was unaware of the accusations in his eyes.

They both sat silently for a while, Michael did not speak, and he glared until she began to talking to him, "Your father was worried and had asked for you, I told him not to go, but he insisted!" Ruth ran to Michael's side by the chair, dropping next to him. However, it was too late, Michael felt as if his soul had left his body and he had become a shell of a man. "I want you out of here, I want a divorce!" Michael threw the glass of scotch at the fireplace; he was livid at her actions and behavior.

Michael got up and left the room, he was tired physically and mentally. Ruth sat there in silence for a few hours silently weeping until she got up to join Michael in bed, he laid there in a peaceful sleep, and she sat and watched him. "There is no way that I am giving up that easily!" Ruth kissed his lips, she craved this man and yearned for his heart. Ruth carefully undressed Michael and herself, she went down his lean athletic chest slowly kissing, and running her tongue gently over him. Ruth got to his naval and stuck her tongue as if she were kissing his lips; Michael stirred a little but still slept. Getting past his naval, she took his soft penis into her mouth as she swirled it around in her mouth and she could feel him growing harder, so she gripped his hips taking him deeper into her mouth.

Suddenly his hands reached around her head and she looked up at him as she pushed him deeper into her mouth. Michael could not help but to let out a loud pleasing moan. Michael could not help but to want her. After all, she was beautiful and his wife, he picked her up to him kissing her deep and caressing her soft firm breasts. Michael laid her down and suckled her breasts as he slid his hands between her thighs feeling her wetness, He needed her right now, and her soft moans turned him on more than anything did. He placed his head between her thighs; he wanted to taste her and make her beg for mercy. Placing his hands under her thighs, he held her in a tight embrace as he stuck his tongue in her velvet softness lightly nibbling her clit, he could feel her body stiffen as she moaned and begged for sweet release. That turned him on and plunged deep inside of her. He pinned her down as he pounded forcefully against her body, both of them began pulling each other's hair tightly, and biting until they could no longer hold out and they both exploded into ecstasy, and then fell asleep in a lovers embrace.

Finally arriving home, Mona was greeted by Flower Fairy and they helped her and the kids into the tepee. After getting the kids settled, Natalya and Eagle Eye headed to his teepee. Mona was so exhausted and she didn't feel well; she slept for days to rid her of a fever. After recovering, they had a welcome home celebration where Eagle Eye informed everyone that he and Natalya intended on getting married. Everyone cheered and congratulated the couple; Mona stared in awe, "It couldn't get any better than this," she thought.

Daily, Wild Heart spoiled and doted on Mona and the kids. She was in pure bliss loving every minute of it. After the next full moon, they held a wedding for Eagle Eye and Natalya; it was hard for them to stay chaste until they were married. Since they were both virgins, their wedding night went quick. However, they were satisfied and kept going at it like rabbits; no one saw them for days.

Ruth was not feeling her best and called for the doctor. After he had visited with Russell and to Michael's surprise, she was with child. Michael was overjoyed that he could finally experience this, as his brother, Dennis and Blue Star, had welcomed a baby girl, Abigail, to the Russell family. Finally, Michael would know the joy of parenthood. Nothing could take this joy out of his heart and so he decided to forgive Ruth and give his marriage a real shot. Michael was a great husband throughout her pregnancy, doting on Ruth and she loved every minute of it. Finally, he was giving her real love that she had desired and longed for. No one had spoken of the past, as if it did not exist. From time to time, Michael imagined what life with Mona would have been like, but he knew in his heart that this way was for the best. However, he did not love her any less and deep in the middle of nowhere there was a memory in his mind, he was after all her first love. Both were with families and they accepted their fates but cherished each other's memory.

The big day had finally arrived for Ruth to give birth and Michael stayed with her up until he was no longer allowed to be at her side. The birth was rough, and Michael sat there anxiously waiting, scared because the midwives had to call the doctor in.

Michael demanded to know what was going on. "A breech birth Sir," one of the midwives said as she was scrambling for more supplies for the doctor. After a few hours, you could hear the wailing of the small child and one of the midwives ran out to him, "It is a boy Sir," but her face was distraught and disheartened. "What's wrong? I want to see my wife!" Michael demanded. Just then, the doctor came out to speak with him. "Michael, your wife is not in good condition and she is asking for you," he motioned for Michael to enter. He goes in cautiously not sure of the sight he would walk into. Michael walked in to blood everywhere; he rushed to the baby, "He is fine Sir," the doctor directed him to Ruth. Tears filled her eyes; she was scared, and he rushed to grip her hand "What is wrong Doc?" Michael was scared. Hanging his head down, "During birth the baby was breech, she had massive tearing; we cannot stop the bleeding, there is too much hemorrhaging." The doctor left so Michael could have his last moments with his wife. Michael had finally loved her as she loved him, "I love you, and I am sorry." He kissed her head and hugged her tightly. Ruth placed her hand on his cheek, "I love you more," her hand fell in slow motion and in that moment, her life departed like the wind. Michael sat there for hours by her side; "He had finally given his full heart, and this is what he had gotten in return," he thought. As he sat grieving for his dead wife, he was called by his brother Dennis; their father's health had been going up and down until this moment and he had asked for Michael. Russell sat up waiting for Michael to enter the room. "I hear congrats are in order on your son," Russell coughed up and laughed at the same time. Michael was confused at his father's behavior, "I guess you heard that Ruth died giving birth."

He was still very upset about it. "Took that whore long enough to be caught by fate," Russell spit up blood. "I was hoping she'd go before me," he chuckled. Michael was confused, "How can his father be so cruel at a time like this?" he thought. Michael went to see his dying father, but Dennis stopped him. "Son, that baby could be anybody's; hell it could be mine!"

Michael could not believe what he was hearing but his bother held him back from attacking their father. "Michael, dad isn't lying," Dennis told his brother. "You knew and said nothing?" Michael broke away from his brother, "You two are real pieces of work, stay away from my son!" Michael stormed out as the hate and anger ran through his veins.

CHAPTER 13

Michael loathed his father but forgave his brother; he let his emotions fester for months, and Russell stayed bed ridden because his health never improved. Michael devised a plan to get even with his father. That night Michael took his father dinner, apologized for overacting, and forgave him for sleeping with his wife. Russell ate his food while he listened to Michael speak about family bonds and forgiveness. Michael and Russell laughed and enjoyed each other's company as a father and son should have, they stayed up to the wee hours of the night.

Michael poured them a glass of scotch and they toasted each other. Russell guzzled it down; Michael immediately poured him another and they toasted each other again. The last and final glass Michael poured for himself and he told his father, "You shouldn't drink too much." Russell laughed as he slowly laid back to rest. Michael insisted on playing a song for his father so he played one of his favorite tunes. Russell started to cough profusely and choke while Michael turned up the music. Walking to his father's, side he leaned in his ear, "Now who's laughing? Enjoy your last moments." He softly chuckled at his father while looking him in the eye so he could watch the suffering on his face.

Michael had laced his father's glass with Arsenic. Everyone knew that he had forgiven his father and he knew no one would suspect him. His father was dying anyway. Michael stood up as he watched his father struggle to breathe. As his father took his last breath, he told him, "Forgive me as I have forgiven you!" He restarted the record, turning the volume down and turning off the lights as he shut the door, leaving his father to die alone. Michael felt all the cruelty his father had done to others throughout the years; he deserved every minute of his painful fate. Michael also felt as if he were helping himself as well; he was never going to recover from his bed. He had to forgive Russell and put him out of his misery. all in one night.

Mona and Wild Heart had some great years together; they ended up with six children and raised them with Natalya and Eagle Eye's children. Life was good until the fever swept over them. Their two youngest girls and Wild Heart had caught the fever and had to be quarantined. Mona stayed at their sides, tending to their every need. The baby girls were the first in the village to die and with that, Wild Heart slowly lost his will. Mona stayed at his side begging and pleading for him to fight. "I cannot be without you," she wept on his chest. "Please don't lose your will, I love you." Mona held his hand and he let go as he took his last breath. It swept past her cheek as she cried; and a big piece of his soul died that day and she begged the gods to take her too, so she could be with her beloved. Mona sat in silence for months mourning and suffering the loss of her love and her babies. The other children were almost at adulthood so she left them with Natalya and Eagle Eye; she could not stomach being there without him. She felt as though she were being punished for loving him too much. She decided she would roam until she died; nothing else mattered. Her kids understood and gave their blessings. Mona had a once in a lifetime love, her mind was distraught and her body weak as she prayed for death; she did not want her kids seeing her die, their father's death was enough.

Mona had found a small place on an edge of a town and she decided on the spot she would die; she would sit there until death came to take her to her beloved. Weeks passed as she stayed there, her health deteriorated. Finally, a stranger passed by seeking shelter from a storm so as her last act of good will before death, she weakly peeled the door open to help the stranger. She thought that if she was lucky maybe he'd kill her, breaking her curse. As Mona opened the door and all the color left her face. There in front of her, stood Michael. They stared at one another in silence for a long moment.

Michael saw that Mona was in bad shape. In shock she almost fell to her knees, but he caught her and picked her up shutting the door. "Are you alright?" he sat her down on her bed making her comfortable. "I am fine" she lied looking down, "You don't look fine, where is Wild Heart?" his eyes searched the room. Mona broke out in tears, "He is gone!" she could not hold back her tears; they stung her face like hot coals. Michael tried to console her, but it was impossible, she was in no shape to talk and then she started to babble and speak incoherently. After a few hours he finally got her to rest, he laid beside her on the floor, but he held her hand throughout the night never letting go. When Mona opened her eyes, she felt someone holding onto her hand and she looked over hoping it had been a dream and that it was Wild Heart. Looking at Michael sleeping at her side comforted her but made her sad; all she wanted was to hold Wild Heart's hand. Mona did not let his hand go but squeezed it tighter; somehow, it made her feel closer to Wild Heart. She laid there and silently cried for forgiveness from Wild Heart for holding Michael's hand. She had felt no comfort since his death and her body yearned for Wild Heart, for her soul was already gone with his.

Mona waited for Michael to wake up and move; she did not want to let his hand go. When Michael sat up he apologized, "I am sorry" and he pulled his hand back, "Please, not yet!" she held onto it. "Can you tell me what happened?" He placed his other hand on top of her hand "Wild Heart and our two youngest girls died from the fever." She couldn't help but cry. Scrambling to his feet he sat next to her and held her as she cried some more. "I will always be around if you need me," he wiped her tears. "I don't want to be you and your wife's burden," she sobbed. "Mona, she died in child birth," he hugged her. Mona looked up confused, "Wow look at us, how did we end up like this?" Mona slowly left his embrace but Michael held onto her hand as well. "Michael, I can't replace my love." She let his hand go, "And I am not asking you to!" He reached back for her hand.

They spent the next few days catching up without any worries or pressures from the outside world. "Can we just stay like this?" Michael asked her. "I know I cannot have your heart, but you are still my best friend. We have both suffered and yet, still find comfort in one another," he looked her with pleading eyes. "Michael, I await death to join Wild Heart and my children." She looked away, "Can I wait with you? I just don't want to be alone." Michael grabbed her hand. "I want nothing more from you than your companionship and company until our last days," Michael hugged her, and she accepted. Michael left to go home and get a few things but decided to return within a week to spend their last days together. After Michael left, Mona felt a little guilt at allowing another man into her life, but she kept her word upon his return a week later. They had the best few months together, one night they decided to have a big meal with drinks. Mona turned to Michael, "My life now feels complete." As they laid down holding hands to sleep side-by-side, as they always did. The following morning as they awoke he had a surprise for Mona. He went to kiss her cheek and it was cold. As Michael began to shake her, there was still no response. He pulled her head upon his lap and wept silently as he kissed her one last time.

Mona had died in her sleep, peacefully and with a smile.

ABOUT THE AUTHOR

Yasmine Russell was born in Toledo, Ohio in 1979 to parents Ruth and Michael. Yasmine then moved to a very small town, Media, Ill in 1993 with her mother, stepfather and three of her younger siblings. Yasmine attended Southern Jr. High School and Southern High School where she graduated in 1998. Yasmine developed a taste for history and learning about other cultures during her school years. Yasmine joined the National Guard at 17 with her best friend for two years to figure out life and evolve as a young woman. Growing up tomboyish, Yasmine held jobs such as a Technician at Valvoline to an Assistant Manager for a gas station. Yasmine also joined the Naval Reserves for almost six years, and received a release to go Active Army where she was an 88M. Life was not always kind, but she always found her way through the journey. Yasmine possesses an associates degree in social work, and is working towards a bachelor's degree in business. Yasmine has worked the last six years for one of the biggest names in the automobile industry and regularly travels the world when the opportunity presents itself. Yasmine has two daughters and takes care of her great nephew. Yasmine is a dreamer with an active imagination, who loves helping others. Yasmine loves to love; fitting with this, Yasmine hopes that you will enjoy getting lost in the pages of this amazing love filled journey.